SANTA, SURF

and

SAPPHIRES

EMERALD FINN

FINESSE SOLUTIONS

Cover design by Wicked Good Book Designs
Published by Finesse Solutions Pty Ltd
2022/12
ISBN: 9781925607116

Author's note: This book was written and produced in Australia and uses
British/Australian spelling conventions, such as "colour" instead of
"color", and "-ise" endings instead of "-ize" on words like "realise".

A catalogue record for this book is available from the National Library of
Australia

For all the friends who cheered me on.

CHAPTER 1

Opening your door to find a policeman on the doorstep usually means trouble of some sort has come calling. But in this case, the only danger was to my heart.

Curtis Kane was a fine specimen of manhood—ridiculously tall and with a muscular build that any professional footballer would envy. Not to objectify him or anything, but Curtis in uniform, with his navy blue shirt stretched tight across his wide chest, was a sight that until now I had thought was the pinnacle of masculine beauty. I guess I had a thing for men in uniform.

Only now, as the sight of him smiling on my doorstep did strange things to my insides, I realised there was something better than Curtis in uniform, and that was Curtis in a dinner suit.

"Hi," I said, as breathless as a teen on her first date. In my defence, our relationship was very new—so new, in fact, that tonight's ball was our first official outing as a couple. So I thought a little breathlessness was understandable.

"Hi," he said in that deep baritone of his. "You look beautiful."

"Thanks." I was wearing my only full-length ball-gown, which was a deep sapphire colour that brought out the blue of my eyes. My hair was up in a loose bun that allowed little tendrils to curl around my face, and I even had on a full face of makeup. It seemed like overkill for a sleepy little town like Sunrise Bay, but Aunt Evie had assured me that the annual Yule Ball was a Big Deal and formalwear was expected.

Curtis leaned in to kiss me, but just as our lips touched, Rufus finished wolfing down his kibble and realised there was someone at the door. He came barrelling down the hall and pushed past me to hurl himself joyfully on Curtis. It was a measure of Curtis's strength that he didn't stagger under the onslaught of thirty kilos of enthusiastic golden retriever.

"Hey, boy." He grinned, his dimple peeking out as he patted Rufus, and my heart did another little flip. As well as uniforms, I was also a sucker for a man with a dimple. "I'm happy to see you, too."

"I'm sorry." I tried to shove Rufus out of the way. "He's not usually so boisterous. He's getting hair all over your pants."

"It's fine," Curtis said, brushing ineffectually at the offending hair.

"I'll get a clothes brush."

"Don't worry about it. We'd better head off, I'm a little

late, sorry. Had to drop Maisie at Mum's." He treated me to another display of that heart-stopping dimple. "She wanted to come along and see you all dressed up. I had to promise to take a photo of you instead. Hope that's okay."

Maisie was his six-year-old daughter and one of my favourite people in my new home town of Sunrise Bay. She had her father's chocolate-brown eyes and dark hair, though hers fell in curls past her shoulders, unlike his short, military-style cut. She was cute as a button and full of opinions on the world, all of which she was happy to share.

"Of course. I'm the last person in the world to object to having my photo taken." I'd started a photography business when I'd moved to Sunny Bay, as it was affectionately known, so photos were my bread and butter. In fact, I'd promised Aunt Evie to take some tonight. She was on the organising committee for the ball and had been working hard for weeks to pull it all together. "I'll just grab my camera bag."

Rufus gave me a betrayed look when he realised he wasn't coming with us. I promised him an extra-long walk in the morning as we left.

The ball was being held at the Metropole, a grand old hotel, only slightly past its prime, that perched on the southern headland and enjoyed a stunning view across Sunrise Bay. It was still light outside, courtesy of daylight saving, when we pulled up, but the place was lit up like a Christmas tree for the occasion. Lights were strung along the second-floor balconies and a giant wreath hung over the main doors. Someone had even rolled out a red carpet, and I felt like a movie star as I walked along it side by side with Curtis. Even in my high heels he towered over me, but he matched his stride to mine. Hot *and* considerate. He was the complete package.

Inside, we climbed the grand, sweeping staircase to the ballroom, which was festooned with tinsel and enormous red baubles. A huge number of people mingled inside, and more were coming in all the time. Everyone looked far more glamorous than I was used to seeing the good citizens of Sunny Bay. Gone were the shorts and T-shirts, replaced by satin and lace, bowties and fancy jewellery. Diamonds flashed at women's throats and dangled from their ears. I glanced around the huge room, dazzled, searching for someone I recognised.

I spotted Aunt Evie at the front of the room, talking to a woman in a daringly backless gown, and started to make my way through the crowd. Heads turned as we passed, and many people greeted Curtis. I took a gleeful satisfaction in being with the handsomest man in the room.

In fact, I figured I'd earned a night of celebration after the stress of the last few weeks. Sleepy Sunny Bay had been rocked by murder recently, and I'd been up to my armpits in alligators trying to ensure the crimes didn't go unpunished. Finally, I could put all that behind me and just relax and focus on my own life.

"Everyone's looking at you," Curtis murmured in my ear as we wove through the crowd. "You're the most beautiful woman in the room."

I was pretty sure that *he* was the reason people were

staring, not me, but it was sweet that he thought so. I was blushing as we reached Aunt Evie.

Her eyes, as blue as mine, lit with a smile. "Look at you two! Don't you make a handsome couple!" She kissed my cheek, then beckoned imperiously for Curtis to bend down far enough so that she could reach his. Aunt Evie was tiny, and looked like a child next to my towering date, but what she lacked in size, she made up for with an outsized personality.

"You look very nice yourself," I told her. "That colour suits you."

She was wearing an emerald-green gown with a high neck and simple flowing lines. She had forsaken her usual style of enormous earrings in favour of a pair of emerald studs, and looked very elegant.

"Thank you, darling. I scrub up all right for an old girl."

I kissed the woman in the glamorous backless dress, too, since it turned out to be my friend Priya. From behind and with her hair up, I hadn't recognised her. Smoky eyeshadow made her dark eyes look even bigger than usual, and her gown was the deep red of fine wine.

"Don't look now, but Mum's headed this way," she said, glancing over my shoulder. "She's busting to ask you about Jack."

I stiffened, feeling like a deer caught in the headlights. "What do I say?"

Jack was my new next-door neighbour. He was a nurse and therefore perpetually sleep-deprived, which was the only reason I could see for him agreeing to pretend to be

Priya's boyfriend at an upcoming family dinner. It sounded like a sure-fire road to disaster to me, but Priya was determined to stop her mother's constant matchmaking, and this was what she'd come up with.

"Just give her a quick answer and change the subject. Don't look at me like that! You'll be fine."

"But I'm a terrible liar."

"You don't have to lie. Just tell her what a stand-up guy he is."

"But what if she asks me when you started going out or something?"

"Relax. Sshh. Here she comes."

Why did people always tell you to relax when they'd just done something to stress you out? I scowled at Priya, who grinned back, completely unrepentant. Then I smoothed my expression into a polite smile as a tall woman with Priya's beautiful dark eyes joined us.

I'd met Amina once before—thankfully before the whole dating deception scheme was hatched. She was a doctor, and Aunt Evie had taken me to see her after my car accident.

Amina was warm and caring and very intelligent. Combined with her persistence in getting to the root of a patient's problem, that made her a great doctor. But those traits also made her hard to fool, and I was quaking just a little in my sparkly high heels as she smiled at me.

"Charlie!" She put her hand on my arm and gave it a friendly squeeze. "You must tell me all about this new neighbour of yours."

Yep. That was Amina. Straight to the point. I caught Priya's eye.

"Anyone want another drink?" Priya asked, giving me a wink before she sauntered off towards the bar.

That traitor. *She* was the one who'd concocted this wild scheme. The least she could do was stick around while I played unwilling accomplice. Faced with Amina's expectant smile, I felt as guilty as if the whole thing were my idea.

"Oh, he's a great guy," I said weakly, watching Priya lean confidently on the bar and say something that made the bartender laugh. "He, um. Loves animals."

Amina frowned. "What about his job? Does he have good prospects?"

Clearly she wasn't interested in hearing about Jack's cat Sherlock, or how Jack lavished attention on Rufus every time he came over, although in my book, "loves animals" was a much higher recommendation than "has a high-paying job". I'd learned that lesson quite thoroughly from my ex-and-not-at-all-lamented fiancé.

"He's a nurse," I said, casting a desperate glance over her shoulder at her daughter, who was still chatting happily with the bartender and showing absolutely no signs of coming to save me. "You should have a lot in common."

"Yes, but what about his family? Is he a religious person?"

"Emily, there you are!" Aunt Evie cried. Amina was forced to leave off the interrogation long enough to greet Emily and her parents.

They were joining us at Aunt Evie's table tonight, and I'd never been more glad to see anyone. I knew Priya would never let me hear the end of it if her mother discovered the deception because of me. Since I wasn't known for my poker face, I was terrified of giving the game away. Lying to people made me downright nervous.

I hadn't met the elder Chens before. Mrs Chen was about Aunt Evie's height, with the ageless beauty so many Chinese women seemed to possess. She could just as easily have been Emily's older sister as her mother, with her unlined face and jet black hair. Mr Chen at least had a few grey hairs. He was a little taller than his wife and very smiley. Emily introduced them as Pim and Gregory.

"You're Emily's friend who solved those murders," Gregory said, smiling. "Very good job!"

Pim nodded decisively, then slanted a mischievous look at Curtis. "She will put you out of business."

"I keep telling her to become a detective." Curtis smiled, a teasing light in his warm brown eyes. "But for some reason she prefers taking photos to catching killers."

"Very sensible," Pim said approvingly. "Running her own business is much better than chasing criminals."

Emily laughed. "Mum loves an entrepreneur."

"No laughing," her mum said. "Business paid your school fees."

Emily rolled her eyes. "I didn't want to go to that posh school anyway," she told me in a stage whisper. I could tell this was an old argument between them—well, it had to be. Emily must have finished school at least a decade ago.

"Ungrateful child," her mother said with a fond smile. "What did I do to deserve such an ungrateful child?"

Curtis and I chatted to Emily and Pim until it was time to take our seats. I breathed a sigh of relief when Amina went to her own table. Priya didn't rejoin us until her mother was safely out of the way, I noted.

"That drink took an awfully long time to get," I said when she sat down on Curtis's other side. "Very slow bartender, is he?"

"We got chatting," Priya said, grinning. Clearly she felt no shame at abandoning me in my hour of need.

"Pretty *cute* bartender, you mean," Emily said. She was sitting on my left, with her dad and then her mum on the other side of her.

Pim looked up and followed the direction of Emily's gaze. The bartender looked somewhere between thirty and maybe thirty-five, with a powerful build that suggested he worked out a lot. His hair was cut in a trendy style, very short on the sides and long in the front. He was also rather handsome.

"He looks like a nice Chinese boy," Pim said. "You should talk to him, Emily."

"You can't tell from the other side of the room whether someone is a nice boy, Mum."

Pim turned to Priya. "Is he nice?"

"Very," Priya said.

Pim smirked triumphantly at Emily, who made a sound of exasperation in her throat.

"You're as bad as Priya's mum."

"You don't have to marry him," Pim said. "Just talk.

You never know what might happen. Although ... there *is* mistletoe hanging over all the balcony doors."

"Hear that, Charlie?" Priya asked. "There's mistletoe everywhere. And you know what that means ..."

I felt heat roar into my cheeks and looked down. Yeah, right. I had plans for my first real kiss with Curtis, and they didn't involve a crowd of eager onlookers.

"What are we all talking about?" Aunt Evie asked, having finished her conversation with a couple passing by.

Oh, no. I was *not* mentioning the word mistletoe in front of my aunt. She didn't need me to give her ideas.

"I saw a fun quiz online the other day." I just blurted the first thing that came into my head. "One of the questions was 'What would you post on social media that was so unlike you that all your friends would know you were being held hostage?'"

"That's easy," Priya said. "I'd say I was desperate to get married."

"Your mother would think all her prayers had been answered," Emily said.

"Yeah, but the rest of you would know to call the cops."

Aunt Evie frowned. "I'm not sure I could be that clever in an emergency. I'd probably just put something like *coconut coconut*."

I laughed. "People would think you were having a stroke, not being held hostage."

"Well, at least they'd send an ambulance."

"Is Heidi coming tonight?" Curtis asked me, nodding at the two vacant seats at our table.

"No." I smiled up at him, grateful for the change of subject. "She said she's putting in such long hours at the shop at the moment that she was too tired for a big night out midweek."

Heidi was one of my closest friends in Sunny Bay. She was a bubbly person with enormous amounts of energy, but even she had her limits. She owned Toy Stories, a lovely little shop in town where she sold toys and children's books.

Curtis nodded. "This must be her busiest time of year."

"Yeah. Apparently she sells more in the week before Christmas than in any other whole month."

"I can't believe it's almost Christmas," Emily said. "Where has this year gone?"

"I know, right?" I said. This had been a big year for me. I'd gotten engaged, planned a wedding, broken the engagement and cancelled the wedding, then uprooted my whole life and moved to Sunrise Bay. A *very* big year.

I glanced at the gorgeous man beside me. I was pretty pleased with how things had turned out, actually.

"Wait until you're my age," Aunt Evie said from across the table. "Whole decades fly past in the blink of an eye. I swear this time last year, I was still young and beautiful."

"Seventy-two isn't old," I said. "And you're still beautiful."

"I bet you just scored yourself an extra Christmas gift with that comment," Andrea said, appearing at the table with her friend Nick in tow. She smiled at us as they settled in the empty seats between Aunt Evie and Priya. "Hi everyone, sorry we're late."

She was wearing a black satin dress with a plunging neckline and a pair of diamante earrings that sparkled like mini chandeliers when she turned her head. Nick fiddled with his bowtie as he said hello, as if it were uncomfortable. Considering he normally lived in T-shirts and shorts, he probably wasn't used to such formal attire.

The residents of Sunny Bay had done themselves proud. We could have been in any high-class hotel in Sydney, rubbing shoulders with the rich and famous. I wondered briefly if Curtis's ex-wife Kelly was coming— she *was* rich and famous, at least in Sunny Bay terms. She was the closest thing to a celebrity that the town had.

Hopefully not. The one time we'd met, she'd been downright rude. I was glancing around surreptitiously when a woman in a sequinned gown walked past. She was an older lady, perhaps Aunt Evie's age or a touch younger, and she gave Aunt Evie a little wave, as if she were the queen acknowledging her subjects. Several large rings on her fingers flashed in the light.

"Hello, Evelyn. You've done a marvellous job, as usual. Everything looks lovely."

"Thanks, Geraldine." Aunt Evie plastered a smile on her face, though I knew how much she hated being called by her full name.

"Who was that?" I asked when she'd gone.

"Geraldine Winderbaum," Aunt Evie said. "Insufferable woman, but at least she's generous with her husband's money."

"Which one?" Andrea asked drily. "She's had a few."

Aunt Evie grinned. "All of them. She's donated one of her necklaces for the auction tonight. I think it was a gift from the despised second husband. It's the most enormous sapphire you've ever seen in your life."

"Well, her loss is the hospital's gain, then," Andrea said.

The Yule Ball always included an auction, with the proceeds donated to the local hospital. This year the money was going towards funding new equipment for the children's ward.

Geraldine was at the next table over, seated between a pair of men with matching beer bellies and bored looks on their faces.

"That's her son," Aunt Evie said, following the direction of my gaze. "From her first marriage. Phil Goblin or Goodchild or something. I can never remember."

"Gottwig," Andrea said with a smile.

The guy in question had very little hair and looked to be in his mid-forties.

"Is that his dad on Geraldine's other side?"

Aunt Evie laughed. "As if Geraldine and Ray could be in the same room without coming to blows. No, that's Irving. He's husband number four."

"He's the richest one yet," Andrea said. "She trades up every time."

"Smart woman," said Priya. "I need to do that."

"Then you could forget this thing with Jack," I said, after checking that Priya's mother was nowhere in earshot.

Aunt Evie's ears pricked up. "There's a thing with Jack? Why was I not informed?"

"Not a real one," I said, giving Priya a disapproving look. "She's pretending to be going out with him to get her mother off her back about getting married. He's going with her to a family dinner this Saturday." Only three days away now. If I were Priya I'd be beside myself with nerves by now, but she was perfectly relaxed.

"Just like in a romance novel!" Aunt Evie said with a delighted grin.

"Except without the falling in love afterwards part," Priya added helpfully. "And for goodness' sake don't tell everyone, Charlie, or Mum will find out."

"I'm not telling *everyone*. Just Aunt Evie."

"I heard, too," Curtis pointed out gravely. "And I'm duty bound to uphold the law."

"There's no law against telling a little white lie to your mother," Priya said, horrified. She could probably see her whole house of cards coming down around her ears.

Curtis broke into a grin, unable to keep a straight face any longer. "Just teasing you."

"Well, I hope it doesn't come back to bite you." Aunt Evie shook her head. "Lies have a way of coming out, you know. We mothers can sniff one out a mile away. It's our superpower."

CHAPTER 2

Entrée was delicious, and main course was even better. Whoever the Metropole's chef was, he was a genius with chicken. Our table was one of the first to be served, so after I'd finished my meal, I excused myself and went off to take some photos.

"I know it's a night for you to enjoy yourself," Aunt Evie had said to me a few days earlier. "So I don't want you to spend the whole time taking photos—especially not when you have that gorgeous policeman to keep you busy. But just a few snaps of the important donors would be such a help. And maybe some of the general atmosphere. Priya's going to do a big write-up in the paper and it's good for the Yule Ball's reputation to make it seem like *the* big event of the year, you know?"

I'd said I understood perfectly, and it was no trouble to capture some good shots of the evening. Curtis and Nick were happily chatting about football, so I slipped off to fulfil my promise to Aunt Evie.

First stop was at Geraldine Winderbaum's table. She seemed happy to pose with her husband, especially after I told her that I was taking photos of "the important donors". I could practically see her preening her sequinned feathers at the suggestion that she was important.

"Now get one of the whole family, dear," she said, gesturing for her son to lean into the shot. "Come on, Philip. Victoria, you, too. Where's Flick?"

Philip and Victoria, who I assumed was his wife, dutifully shuffled their chairs closer, though Philip looked as though he was about to expire of boredom.

"I think she went to the bathroom," Victoria said. "Oh, there she is."

A very attractive woman in her thirties wearing a tightfitting red dress with a slit up one side approached the table. Her long black hair rippled down her back in a silken wave almost to her butt, and I was immediately envious. My own hair had never looked that sleek.

Geraldine waved to catch her attention. "Hurry up, Flick, we're having a family photo."

Flick had dark eyes with a slightly Asian look and golden skin quite different to the pale tones of the rest of the family. Perhaps I'd got it wrong and *she* was Philip's wife. But she slid into the vacant seat on the other side of Geraldine, who pulled her closer with a proprietary arm around her bare shoulders.

"You've been gone for ages, darling," Geraldine said. "Where were you?"

"Just stretching my legs."

"You've been smoking again, haven't you?" Phil said. Victoria flapped her hands uselessly, as if to wave away his words. The look of dread on her face suggested the family had a habit of nasty squabbles.

Flick's eyes narrowed. "When I want your opinion, I'll ask for it."

"It's very bad for you," Geraldine said, which I thought was sensible of her until she added, "You know it will give you awful wrinkles."

"Don't start, Mum."

So this was Geraldine's daughter. Aunt Evie had mentioned a few ex-husbands. One of them must have been Chinese. Their daughter was stunning, but there was a sulky set to her mouth as the family posed for their photo.

"Everyone smile," I said cheerily, but there was no coaxing a smile out of Flick—or Phil, for that matter. I gave it up as a bad job and moved on to the next table.

"Charlie," Amina cried when I arrived at her table a little later. "Just the person I want to talk to. I was just telling everyone about Priya's new boyfriend."

"I'd love to chat," I said, which was a bare-faced lie, "but I've got to keep going. Aunt Evie's got me working hard."

I'd never taken a group photo faster—I couldn't wait to get away. I'd be so happy when Priya's stupid family dinner was over. Amina could ask Jack and Priya all the questions she liked on Saturday night and then I might be able to look her in the eye again without feeling like a naughty child.

The waiters started to bring the dessert out. I hurried to the last table, where Delia Backhouse and some others I recognised from my recent dealings with the local police were seated.

"Hi, Charlie." Delia looked very different out of uniform. Her short dark hair framed a face that looked far more glamorous than usual. It occurred to me that I'd never seen her wearing makeup before—or a dress.

"Hi there! You look fantastic."

"Thanks." She gestured at the camera in my hands. "You working tonight?"

"Unofficially. I'm just taking a few snaps to help Aunt Evie out. She's on the organising committee for the ball. Mainly I'm just here to enjoy myself."

"I see you managed to persuade Curtis to come along. Funny, when I asked him if he wanted a ticket for the Yule Ball he said no."

"He was a very late addition. We were only meant to be a table of eight, but Aunt Evie said we could squeeze one more in. The benefits of having an aunt on the committee."

"Hmmm. But it doesn't explain how getting all dressed up to eat expensive food suddenly became a lot more appealing. He seemed quite horrified at the idea when *I* asked him."

I stumbled around for an answer until she laughed and laid a hand on my arm. "I'm only teasing. I haven't seen him this happy in a long time. I'm thrilled for the both of you."

"Thanks." I could feel a blush creeping up my cheeks

and hurried on to taking the photo. I really liked Delia, but it felt so weird to be the centre of attention like this. I'd been so long in my previous relationship that I'd forgotten what it was like to start a new one and have everyone who knew you hanging on every little detail.

I was still a little flustered when I got back to my own table, but one slow smile from Curtis soon set me to rights. I slid into the chair next to him, feeling oddly like I was coming home. Already, he felt like "my person".

I glanced down at the pear tart on the table in front of me. It looked delicious. A sticky date pudding absolutely swimming in butterscotch sauce sat in front of Curtis.

"You didn't want dessert?" I asked as I picked up my spoon, ready to dig in.

"I wasn't sure which one you'd prefer, so I waited," he said. "If you want the sticky date pudding, I'm happy to swap."

Good heavens, could the man be any more perfect?

"That was so thoughtful of you." Warmth filled me. "But I'm happy with this one—unless *you* want it?"

Priya snorted. "You two are going to nice each other to death. Hurry up and eat. The auctions are starting soon."

"I'm not sure I'm talking to you," I said as I cut into the pear tart. "I just had to run from your mother again. She's relentless."

She grinned. "Welcome to my life. That's Indian mothers for you."

"I don't think that's limited to *Indian* mothers," Emily said, with a meaningful sidelong glance at her own mum.

"What?" Pim asked, catching the glance. "What did I do?"

"So many things," Emily said with a laugh. "Soooo many."

"Bah. Why are you still sitting here, anyway?" She nudged Emily's ribs. "You should be over there talking to that nice boy."

We all glanced towards the bartender again. He was really very handsome—he could have been the romantic lead in any romcom movie.

"We need to find out who he is," Aunt Evie said in a conspiratorial tone.

"I'm surprised you guys don't know him," I said to Emily.

"Why?" she asked. "I don't know every Chinese person in Sunny Bay."

"He can tend my bar any time," Emily's mum said, getting out of her chair.

"Mum! Where are you going?"

Pim gave her an innocent look. "Just to get a drink."

Emily groaned. "Don't you dare give him my number."

A feedback whine from the microphone made us all flinch. A grey-haired man was standing on the small stage at the front of the room, leaning apologetically into the microphone.

"Sorry about that, folks. I hope you've enjoyed your desserts. We'll be starting the serious part of the night in a moment, so get your wallets ready. We have a whole host of great items for you to bid on, courtesy of our generous sponsors—and every dollar will be going to the Sunrise Bay Community Hospital. Dig deep, folks!"

"Who's he?" I asked my aunt.

"Jeff Borello," she said. "The mayor of the shire."

"Are you bidding on anything, Evie?" Andrea asked.

"I wouldn't mind that voucher to the day spa," Aunt Evie said.

"There might be some fierce competition for that," Andrea said. "I was looking at the holiday to Queensland. I guess it depends on how high the bidding goes."

Pretty high, as it turned out. Someone from Amina's table got the holiday voucher—one of the other doctors from her practice. He looked mighty pleased with himself at the prospect of an all-expenses paid trip for four to the Gold Coast. The auctioneer was also pleased at the price he'd gotten for it. At regular intervals, he announced how much had been raised so far for the hospital, to encourage people to spend up big.

Pim wandered back to the table, having stopped to chat half a dozen times on her way back from the bar.

"He's single," she announced with a triumphant look at Emily.

"I hope you didn't—"

"I didn't give him your number. I told him I have a daughter, very good cook, still single."

Emily groaned and covered her eyes.

Andrea took pity on her and changed the subject. "You've done a great job with the ball this year, Evie. It was a stroke of genius to have it here instead of at the surf club."

"Much more upmarket, isn't it?" Aunt Evie agreed. "I thought it would encourage people to spend more on the auction."

"Didn't it cost more to hire, though?" Priya asked.

"A little, but they gave us a very competitive price," Aunt Evie said. "Seeing as how it was for a good cause. They even did all the decorating for us, so in the end we came out about even."

Andrea gestured at the vase of flowers in the middle of the table. A tall, black cylinder supported branches of soft grey-green eucalyptus and a spray of native flowers in reds and whites. "They supplied these? They must have cost a fortune."

Aunt Evie grinned. "They're fake—very realistic-looking, aren't they?"

Andrea had to reach out and check for herself, because they did indeed look real.

Aunt Evie laughed at the look on her face. "These are their standard decorations, if people don't provide their own. They said it was more economical to buy artificial flowers and store them than to keep getting fresh ones that die. Particularly as artificial flowers these days are so good it's hard to tell they're not real."

Pim congratulated Aunt Evie on her money-saving skills. "More money for the hospital," she added.

"That's what it's all about," Aunt Evie said. "Curtis, are you bidding on anything tonight? There's a very nice necklace coming up later."

"You mean the one that Geraldine donated?" I asked, horrified.

I'd seen it earlier as I went around taking photos, on its display stand on the small stage. It was a pendant featuring a massive sapphire surrounded by diamonds. Rather old-fashioned—it wasn't my taste at all—but it screamed money.

Curtis laughed, making that cute dimple of his peek out. "I don't think a policeman's salary runs to that kind of expense. I'd have to sell my car, and even then I'm not sure I could afford it."

"Maybe one day." Aunt Evie smiled at him. "Oh, look, the auction is starting again."

The mayor was tapping his hammer lightly on the podium in front of him to get everyone's attention. When the buzz of conversation in the room died down, he said, "All righty, folks. Now is the moment we've all been waiting for. We have this exquisite necklace." He gestured at the necklace set up on its stand on one side of the stage. "It's been very generously donated by Mrs Geraldine Winderbaum. How about a round of applause, folks?" He smiled down at her, and she inclined her head graciously.

"It's a Ceylon sapphire of three karats, surrounded by seven small diamonds, three of which are pink Argyle diamonds," he went on. "As you may know, those are among the rarest in the world and very expensive. If you were to buy a piece such as this from a jeweller, it would probably cost you upwards of forty grand." There were several gasps around the room and he nodded, a pleased look on his face. "That's right, forty grand. But tonight, you have the chance to own this piece for something less. Although, let's not make it *too* much less, hey folks?

Remember, every cent of the winning bid will be going towards our hospital's new equipment."

I leaned closer to Curtis, getting a whiff of his heavenly aftershave in the process. The man smelled even better than the pear tart had tasted, and that was saying something. "If it's worth forty grand, why doesn't she sell it and then give that money to the hospital instead? What if it only sells for ten tonight? That's thirty thousand dollars that the hospital misses out on."

"She probably couldn't get anything like that on the second-hand market. Jewellers are like car dealers—they never buy anything for what it's actually worth, because they need to make a profit when they resell."

I nodded. "That makes sense."

"Besides, Jeff is an experienced auctioneer. He must have done a dozen of these charity balls. He knows what he's doing. I guarantee you he will squeeze the last drop out of every bidder."

"Are we ready, folks?" Jeff asked.

A few people in the audience called out, "Yes."

Jeff grinned. "I can't hear you."

"Yes!" the audience roared.

"Let's get down to business, then. Given its value, I'm starting the bidding at ten thousand dollars."

Emily whistled softly. "Ten thousand dollars? Who's got that kind of money?"

"Ten thousand five hundred," called a man at Amina's table.

I glanced at Emily, eyebrows raised. "I guess some people do."

"Oh, pish-tush," Aunt Evie said. "There are plenty of rich people in Sunrise Bay. Think of all those mansions on the headland."

"Eleven thousand," someone called from the back of the room.

That was true. Aunt Evie's retirement village was surrounded by enormous expensive homes, all jostling for the view across the bay from the headland.

"Eleven thousand two hundred."

The auctioneer shook his head almost sadly. "Folks, let's not mess around with a couple of hundred dollars here or there. We're talking about sick children. We're talking about saving lives. What if the life that's saved turns out to be *your* child's?"

"Fifteen thousand," called a man at the table to our left.

"That's more like it," Jeff said. "Who will bid me sixteen?"

Curtis grinned at me. "I told you he was good."

Slowly, the bidding crept up in amounts of five hundred dollars until it reached twenty thousand. I glanced across at the man who currently had the winning bid. It was the same man who had jumped the bidding up to fifteen thousand. He was tall and thin with a shock of fair hair, around forty, but a fit forty. His suit was so nicely tailored to him that it clearly wasn't a hired tux. A thick gold ring flashed on his hand as he raised a glass of champagne to his lips, his gaze resting placidly on the auctioneer, as if twenty thousand dollars didn't mean too much to him.

The silence stretched. "Come on, folks," Jeff said. "Don't stop there! Who will bid me twenty-one?"

The pause stretched longer and longer. It looked like Mr Cool-as-a-Cucumber had bought himself a necklace.

"I will." Phil Gottwig raised his hand, still looking bored.

"He's bidding on his own mother's necklace?" Priya murmured. "What, he can't bear for the peasants to get their hands on it?"

The auctioneer pointed his hammer at Phil. "Thank you, sir."

The words were hardly out of his mouth before the tall, fair-haired man said, "Twenty-two thousand."

I looked over at him again. This was like following a tennis match, with Phil on the table to our right and this other guy to our left. He didn't look placid anymore. In fact, he looked downright peeved.

"Who's that guy?" I asked Curtis, who only shrugged.

Aunt Evie leaned across the table. "That's Stellan Eriksson."

Priya glanced at him, too. "Oh, the architect?"

"That's right," Aunt Evie said. "He went to school with Phil Gottwig. They were best friends."

"Twenty-three thousand," Phil said, giving Stellan a dead-eyed stare.

"Twenty-three thousand five hundred," Stellan replied immediately.

All the other bidders seemed to have dropped out. Phil and Stellan were the only ones left.

"They *were* best friends?" I asked. "As in, they're not

anymore?"

"No," Aunt Evie replied. "There was a big scandal oh, twenty years ago now it must be. They both fell in love with the same girl."

"I remember that," Emily's mum said. "Big scandal. Stellan stole Phil's girlfriend."

"That's what Phil said anyway," Aunt Evie said. "Though Stellan always maintained that Phil and Louisa had broken up before he started going out with her."

I frowned. "Still, if he and Phil were close, he must have realised that jumping in as soon as Louisa became free would upset his best friend."

"Not necessarily," Priya pointed out. "It would depend on why they broke up. Maybe Phil dumped her."

Aunt Evie shrugged. "I don't remember all the details now. It was a long time ago and I only heard about it through a friend who used to play tennis with Geraldine."

The bidding was over twenty-five thousand dollars now and Stellan was staring straight ahead at the auctioneer, a muscle twitching in his jaw. He didn't look happy.

"Seems as though they still haven't got over it, though," I said.

Phil, on the other hand, was sitting back in his seat, one arm hooked over the back of it. He looked remarkably relaxed for someone who was contemplating spending an enormous amount of money on a piece of jewellery. Finally, he looked as though he was enjoying himself. He glanced at Stellan, a small smile playing around his mouth.

"Thirty thousand," he said.

The bid brought a smattering of applause from around the room. The auctioneer grinned in pleasure.

"Thirty thousand. Thank you very much, sir, very generous of you. Any advance on thirty thousand?" He eyed Stellan hopefully.

Stellan gazed back at him, his face rigid. "Thirty-two thousand and that's my final offer."

"And a very fine offer it is too, sir." The auctioneer glanced at Phil, who shook his head regretfully. He raised his hammer and a hush fell across the room. "Thirty-two thousand going once. Twice." He paused, probably for dramatic effect, since it seemed clear that the two bidders had reached the end of their contest. He brought the hammer down. "Sold to Mr Eriksson for thirty-two thousand dollars. Congratulations, sir."

Stellan nodded, face still impassive, as everyone started clapping.

Aunt Evie applauded harder than anyone else in the room. "This is going to be our best year yet, I can feel it. The hospital will be *so* pleased."

"And thanks again to our very generous donor, Mrs Winderbaum," the auctioneer added. "Perhaps we could get you up here to present the necklace to its new owner?"

At the next table, Geraldine rose regally from her seat, taking the applause of the room as her due.

"She is really getting off on this lady of the manor stuff, isn't she?" Priya said.

"I guess she deserves to do a little preening, considering how much money the hospital is getting out of this," I said.

Priya rolled her eyes. "Trust you to have something nice to say about everyone."

"Just think of those lovely beepy hospital machines and keep clapping." I stood up, too. Aunt Evie would undoubtedly want a photo of this.

As Geraldine headed for the stage, I noticed one person who wasn't clapping. Phil seemed to have lost all interest in the auction now that his archenemy had won the necklace. He had his head down, focused on his phone. I supposed he might have been posting on Facebook about what a generous person his mother was, but he was back to looking bored with the whole thing.

I grabbed my camera and went to set up for the photo. Stellan and Geraldine were both on the stage, standing in front of the necklace on its stand.

"Perhaps you could shake hands and look this way, please?"

Stellan bent slightly from his great height and offered one large hand to Geraldine. Then they both turned to smile at me. Geraldine's smile was considerably brighter. In fact, Stellan looked a little green around the gills. Was he already regretting the massive amount of money he'd just spent? From the corner of my eye, I could see Phil still on his phone. Did he really not care that he'd lost the auction, or was he just trying to project that image so he didn't lose face? Perhaps the bored look was his way of telling Stellan how indifferent he was to the outcome.

Well, it was no skin off my nose either way. I lifted the camera, but as my finger tightened on the shutter button, all the lights in the room went out.

CHAPTER 3

THE DARKNESS FILLED WITH SURPRISED SCREAMS AND SOME laughter. Was it a blackout? How odd—there were no storms to cause a power cut. Someone brushed past me in the pitch black, making me jump. For a moment I thought I could smell jasmine. Something sweet, anyway.

"Hold tight, everyone." The auctioneer's voice cut across the chatter in the room. "I'm sure we'll have the lights back on momentarily. If you could all just stay seated until then so we don't have anyone tripping over in the dark, that would be great."

I hadn't appreciated until this moment how very dark it could be in a room without windows. The Metropole's ballroom did have a bank of glass doors that let out onto a rooftop terrace, but they were way down the other end of the room and only seemed to emphasise how very dark it was at this end. In the absence of light, the noises in the room seemed very loud, and I flinched as someone knocked over a glass somewhere close behind me.

A faint light bloomed and I turned towards it. Priya had turned on the torch feature on her mobile phone. A moment later people everywhere were doing the same and you could feel the whole room relax. Nervous laughter and speculation about the blackout rippled around the ballroom. Several men left to investigate.

The lights came back on, leaving everyone blinking at each other in the sudden glare. There were a few cheers, followed by a sudden scream.

"It's gone!" Geraldine shrieked. "The necklace is gone!"

She was still on the stage with Stellan and Jeff, one hand pressed to her chest in shock. The stand between them, where the necklace had been displayed, was empty.

I spun around and snapped three quick photos, trying to cover the whole room, with the vague idea that a record of where everyone was at that moment might prove useful.

A lady at Geraldine's table was dabbing ineffectually at her dress. Someone had knocked over a glass of red wine, which must have been almost full, judging by the size of the stain spread across the white tablecloth.

She wasn't the only one. There were other spillages around the room, as if people had suddenly lost their bearings when the lights went out. One of the waiters was crouched over a mess of dropped cake that had somehow slipped off a plate in the dark. A man at the back of the room was actually on the floor, being helped up by a couple of others from his table. It looked as though he'd been walking between tables when the lights went out and had managed to trip on a chair leg.

A hubbub of voices rose as everyone started talking at once. Stellan moved to the back of the little stage, looking around as if he thought the necklace might somehow have been knocked from its perch and fallen off the back. The auctioneer, looking very pale, banged his hammer for silence.

"Let's all stay calm," he said.

Aunt Evie jumped to her feet. "Stay calm? When thirty-two grand has just disappeared?" She looked at Curtis. "What should we do?"

He got to his feet, laying a reassuring hand on her arm. "We'll handle this."

Across the room, Delia and the other police officers were on their feet, too. They might have been wearing evening dress, but their faces showed that they were now on duty. Delia said something to the officer next to her, a young man with curly red hair. He nodded, and he and another officer moved towards the main doors to the ballroom, where they took up a station. Another of their group headed out the door that led to the bathrooms. Delia herself marched to the front of the room and climbed up onto the stage.

She leaned into the microphone. "Ladies and gentlemen, a serious crime has been committed here. I'm afraid I'll have to ask all of you to bear with me as we conduct a search. I know this isn't the way any of us wanted to spend tonight, but I'm sure you understand what has to be done. Please remain in your seats for now."

She stepped down from the dais and Curtis joined her. "We'd better call the station."

She nodded. "I will, but they'll probably tell us to handle it, since we have half of the team here anyway."

I moved to Aunt Evie's side and urged her back into her seat. She looked so upset.

"I'm sure they'll find it," I said.

She gave me a sceptical look. "What are they going to do? Strip search two hundred people?" She shook her head. "I can't believe anyone could do such a thing. That money was for the hospital! But someone must have planned this. If that blackout was a coincidence I'll eat my hat."

I studied the stage. It was one of those temporary ones made of big hollow blocks shoved together. They were covered with some kind of felt or thin carpet, which meant that anyone moving around on it would have made no noise.

The auctioneer had stepped down and was conferring with Delia, but Geraldine and Stellan still stood there, looking a little lost.

"Unless Stellan's just taken advantage of the blackout to pocket it in the dark," Priya said. "Maybe he decided that thirty-two thousand was too much to pay for it after all."

"Sshh!" I hissed. "He'll hear you."

A woman in the same dove-grey business suit that I'd seen the reception staff wearing had joined Delia and the little gathering around the stage. Stellan was currently turning out his pockets and submitting to a gentle but determined pat-down from Curtis.

"Or maybe it was Geraldine," Priya continued. "Let's face it, they're the two obvious suspects. They were standing right next to it when the lights went out. Who else could get there in time?"

"Well, the auctioneer, for one," I felt compelled to point out. "And probably anyone at one of the front three tables."

"Or one of the waiters who was close to the front," Emily added.

"You may as well accuse me," I said. "*I* was one of the closest people."

"Fine. Any of us could have done it," Priya said cheerfully.

"Well, *I* couldn't," Aunt Evie said, giving her a reproving look. Priya did seem to be unreasonably entertained by the whole situation. She was probably thrilled at the prospect of writing a more interesting story on the annual ball than usual. "If I'd tried clambering around that tiny stage in the dark I probably would have fallen off and broken my ankle."

The woman in the suit had a placating hand on Geraldine's arm. Geraldine's face was stormy, as if she thought the theft had been orchestrated purely to steal her moment in the spotlight.

"Not to mention that you wouldn't dream of ripping off the hospital," I added.

"That, too," Aunt Evie said.

"Who's that?" I asked her, indicating the woman in the suit.

"That's Greta Chalmers. She's the events coordinator here. Lovely girl. Very helpful."

I wouldn't have called her a girl—she was middle-aged, though her figure was trim and there wasn't a sign of grey in her dark hair. She nodded at something that Delia said and headed back towards the doors into the kitchen, passing by our table.

"Oh, Evie," she said, catching sight of Aunt Evie. "What a terrible thing! And after all your work, too."

The funny thing about Aunt Evie was that, no matter how down she might be feeling about something, as soon as someone else needed cheering up, she immediately switched on the positivity.

"Never mind that," she said bracingly. "It's the hospital that's important here. But I'm sure the police will recover the necklace sooner or later. Have you met my niece, Charlie?"

Greta smiled half-heartedly and offered her hand, her thoughts clearly more on the drama of the missing necklace than on introductions. "Nice to meet you, Charlie."

"You, too," I said.

"Your aunt is a powerhouse. She almost singlehandedly organised this whole thing."

"Nonsense," Aunt Evie said, though she looked pleased. "I couldn't have done it without you, Greta. You've been so helpful."

Greta looked back at the little huddle of police at the front of the room, her face troubled. "I wish I could do more to help now. But Delia asked me to assemble the staff in the kitchen, so I'd better get on to that."

"Of course."

Greta hurried away and I turned my attention back to the group on the stage. Curtis had finished patting down Stellan, who was readjusting his jacket rather huffily. He was a tall man, almost as tall as Curtis, though built on a much leaner scale. If he'd been at school with Phil Gottwig, he must be the same age, but he looked a good ten years younger. His blond hair was still thick and he looked fit and tanned, whereas Phil was balding and rather rotund.

It seemed it was now Geraldine's turn to be searched, and she was having none of it. "My good woman," she said to Delia, "it was *my* necklace in the first place. Why on earth would I steal it?"

"In the interests of thoroughness, Mrs Winderbaum, it would be helpful if—"

"Certainly not."

Our whole table had fallen silent, shamelessly eavesdropping on the drama out front. Geraldine's table was watching, too, and Phil shoved his chair back and stomped out to join them.

"You should quit wasting time insulting my mother and get on with your jobs," he said, glaring at Delia.

He wasn't a tall man, but he thrust his bulk aggressively at her. She was unmoved—she dealt with angry men all the time in her job.

"This *is* our job, Mr Gottwig," she said calmly. "Mr

Eriksson and Mayor Borello submitted to a search. It will only take a minute."

Phil glanced at Stellan. "I hope you did a thorough job. I bet it's in his pocket right now."

Stellan stiffened. "Are you calling me a thief?"

"It wouldn't be the first time, would it?"

"Oh, get over it, Phil. It's been twenty years."

Geraldine laid a hand on Phil's arm. "Darling, it's all right." She eyed Curtis, a small, flirtatious smile lingering around her mouth. "Perhaps I wouldn't mind submitting to a search if Officer Kane did it."

Priya made a gagging noise. "She's old enough to be his *mother*."

Aunt Evie grinned at her. "Can you blame her? You have to admit, he's rather delicious."

I shushed them both, but no one was paying any attention to us.

"*I* will be searching the ladies," Delia said firmly. "Officer Kane will search the gentlemen."

"Every woman here just had their dreams dashed," Priya said.

"Priya!"

"What? It's all right for you—you can play *Pat Me Down, Officer* any time you like."

CHAPTER 4

THE POLICE SEARCH TOOK A WHILE, EVEN THOUGH A PAIR OF on-duty officers turned up to join in. None of the ladies got patted down by Curtis or any of the male officers—in fact, no one got patted down other than the three people who'd been on the stage when the necklace disappeared. The men turned out their pockets, but of course there were no pockets in any of the ladies' ballgowns, so the women showed the contents of their purses instead.

Just as well it was a gala event. Everyone had brought tiny little evening bags. Poor Delia would have been there for hours if she'd had to go through the kind of bags that most women toted for everyday use. I showed her my camera bag and told her that I'd felt someone brush past me in the dark. She wrote it down in her notebook, but that was probably more for show than anything. We already knew someone had gotten on to the stage who shouldn't have been there. The fact that they'd brushed past people in the dark was no help at all—if that had even been the thief I'd felt.

I hoped the photos that I'd taken of the room immediately after the lights came back on might prove more useful, and promised to send copies to Delia in the morning.

By the time the police had finished, there was only an hour of the ball left, but the DJ started the music anyway and people got up to dance. Since Curtis was still talking to Delia, I slipped into the chair next to Aunt Evie.

"I'm sorry this has spoiled your night with Curtis," she said.

"Don't worry about it. It's fine."

"I suppose it's an occupational hazard of going out with a police officer."

"It could be worse," Emily said, raising her voice to be heard above the music. "He could be an obstetrician. My sister went out with one for a while, and she could never be sure that he'd actually be available. At any time of the day or night, he could be called to the hospital."

"Babies aren't very good at keeping to schedules," I said. "I take it they broke up?"

"Yes. Mum was devastated. She kept saying, *but he was a doctor*, as if that made up for everything."

Pim overheard and leaned in. "He was a very nice boy, too. Your sister would have been better off with him than that useless one she's with now."

"It's a great worry to parents," Aunt Evie said solemnly, "not being able to pick your children's partners." She glanced at me. "To aunts, sometimes, too. I got off the phone and did a victory dance the day you rang to tell me you'd left that awful fiancé of yours."

I laughed, imagining Aunt Evie jiving around her living room. "I'll admit, Will was a lapse of judgement."

She snorted. "A five-year lapse of judgement. You cost me more grey hairs than both my own children put together."

Aunt Evie's hair had always been the same shade of light brown as mine, but these days she needed a little help from a dye bottle. I leaned in and gave her a kiss on the cheek. "Well, it's lucky you dye your hair, then."

Andrea and Nick were dancing. They seemed to be having a good time, though I had to admit that Nick wasn't a very good dancer. He swayed awkwardly from foot to foot without moving much, as if he were a scarecrow nailed to the spot. Andrea didn't seem to mind too much, as they were keeping up a lively conversation at the same time. Priya went off to dance with one of the doctors from her mother's table, and Emily got up with her dad. Gregory Chen was surprisingly adept, and swept her off into a foxtrot. They made the rest of the people on the dance floor look like amateurs.

And yes, maybe I was a *little* disappointed. I'd pictured myself on that dance floor too, twirling happily in Curtis's arms. But there would be other dates. Besides, Aunt Evie needed cheering up. She still looked very troubled by the loss of the necklace, so I kept up a steady flow of light chatter, telling her all about my latest photography clients and my preparations for my first Christmas in my new home.

"What's Curtis doing for Christmas?" she asked.

"I don't know. We haven't actually discussed it yet."

"Better get a wriggle on. It's only next week."

"I know! Trust me, I know. I still have to think of what to get for him and Maisie." What did six-year-old girls like? I had no idea.

"Maisie shouldn't be a problem. Little kids are easy to buy for."

"I guess so. I'll probably go to Toy Stories and ask Heidi's advice. She'll know what the trends are in kids' toys. I want to get Maisie something she'll really like. Curtis is more of a problem."

"Is he a reader? You could get him a book."

"You can never have too many books, right?"

She smiled. "That's true."

We talked for a while, though the music made it hard to hear. Every time she mentioned something about the theft, I changed the subject to what someone was wearing or who was dancing with whom. I couldn't stop her being upset by the loss of the necklace, but at least I could distract her with more pleasant thoughts for a while. There was nothing Aunt Evie liked more than a nice cozy gossip, and the good citizens of Sunny Bay had given us plenty to talk about tonight, between several very daring outfits and some not-so-subtle canoodling between people who really had no business being together.

Soon it was time to leave. I waited in the upstairs foyer outside the ballroom for Curtis. I hadn't seen him in the last half hour or so, and I wasn't sure if he was taking me home or whether I should hitch a ride with Aunt Evie or one of the girls.

"Well, that was one Yule Ball we'll never forget," Emily said, cheerfully swinging her evening bag on its golden chain as she joined me. "Mum will have a wonderful time at mahjong this week telling all her friends about it."

"I wonder if she'll tell them about that cute bartender she was trying to set you up with?"

"Sshh! He's just over there."

Whoops. I hadn't noticed him. He was standing by the doors as if he were waiting for someone to leave the ballroom.

"Did you ever find out his name?" I asked in a low tone.

Her smile peeped out. "It's Tim."

Tim really was very good-looking. He had a face I'd love to photograph, with very sharp cheekbones, and he held himself with great poise. I wondered if he'd been a dancer. He had that kind of natural elegance common among good dancers. Maybe those muscles weren't from the gym after all.

I grinned back at her. "So you talked to him? What's he like?"

She shrugged. "He seems nice enough. He said he was working again tomorrow night, in the main bar, so I thought I might drop by."

"That will make your mum happy!"

"It's just a *drink*, Charlie. Not a date."

"Well, I hope you enjoy your *drink*."

"He's travelling around Australia. He's just stopped here for a couple of months to earn some money."

That was pretty common among backpackers. They moved around the country, picking up work as they went to cover their expenses. But Tim seemed a little old to be a backpacker.

I glanced at him again, in time to see him straighten in anticipation. Clearly whoever he'd been waiting for was coming. Priya emerged from the ballroom, flushed from dancing, and flapping her purse in front of her face in a futile attempt to fan herself. She waved when she saw us and came over.

But Tim hadn't been waiting for Priya. I was only half listening as Priya began talking to Emily, because apparently Flick Winderbaum was the person Tim had been waiting for. Or whatever her name was. Considering how many times Geraldine had been married, they might not share a surname.

Were Flick and Tim hooking up? There went Emily's chances. But no, the look Flick gave him when he stepped forward to catch her attention wasn't at all lover-like. She jumped and drew her jewelled jacket more firmly around her shoulders, though it was a warm night. As if she were trying to protect herself.

He *was* standing a little too close to her, almost looming over her. They were too far away for me to hear what they were saying, but I saw him pass something to her. It was small, too small for me to see what it was, but the colour drained from Flick's face as she glanced down at it.

"What are you staring at?" Priya asked me.

I glanced her way. "Nothing."

By the time I looked back, Flick was shutting her purse with a decisive snap and the thing, whatever it was, was out of sight.

"They'd make gorgeous babies together," she said, following the direction of my gaze. "They both look like they stepped out of the pages of *Vogue*."

"Mmmm." I wasn't really paying attention. Over her shoulder I'd spotted Geraldine, striding towards the pair with a scowl on her face that could stop traffic. Curiouser and curiouser.

Tim saw her coming, too. He murmured to Flick and left, making a smooth exit in our direction.

"Here comes your dream date," Priya said to Emily, who glared at her.

"Oh, hi!" I said as Tim drew level with us. Geraldine had reached Flick and was now talking very fast to her in a furious undertone.

"Hi." Tim smiled at me in a distracted way. "You're the photographer, right?"

"That's right. I hope you're enjoying Sunrise Bay—I heard you were new in town." I nodded in Flick's direction. "Do you two know each other?"

He didn't look back at her. Perhaps he could feel Geraldine's glare lodged between his shoulder blades. "No. I just noticed she'd dropped an earring, so I gave it back to her."

"That was nice of you. Do you know my friend Emily?"

"Yes, we met earlier." He smiled at Emily, who looked

frozen. "Your mum's a hoot. Maybe I'll see you at the bar some time?"

She nodded. "Yeah. Sure."

"'Night, ladies." He strode off, his long legs carrying him down the stairs and away.

Priya grinned at Emily. "You can breathe again, now."

"Charlie!" Emily wailed. "How could you put me on the spot like that? I couldn't think of anything to *say*."

"Relax," I said. "I think he likes you."

"No, he likes my *mum*."

Priya laughed. "Maybe he has a thing for older women."

I shook my head at her. "Not helpful, Priya."

"Never mind," Priya said, "you'll have plenty of time to think of things to talk about before you see him again."

I looked for Geraldine and Flick, but they'd gone. Tim had said he was giving back an earring Flick had dropped. If that was the case, why had she looked so shocked?

CHAPTER 5

CURTIS'S ARRIVAL DROVE IT FROM MY MIND.

"There you are!" he said. "I'm so sorry about tonight."

"Don't worry about it. It's not your fault."

He ran a hand through his short brown hair and gave me a sheepish look. "The guys are short-staffed tonight, and they want me to stay to finish interviewing the staff."

"It's fine. I can hitch a ride home with Aunt Evie."

"I'll make it up to you, I promise." He leaned in, enveloping me in his fresh, woodsy scent, and kissed me on the cheek.

I smiled up at him. "I'll hold you to that. Now go solve the crime."

"That's more your department, isn't it?" That slow smile of his filled me with warmth. He looked at me as if I were the only person in the busy foyer and I felt nourished by his attention, like a plant turning its leaves to the sun. "Maybe you should be staying instead of me."

"Well ..." I trailed off.

46

"You're already thinking about it, aren't you?"

I shrugged one shoulder in an off-hand way. Just because I'd gotten lucky and solved some murders didn't mean I was suddenly a professional detective. "Of course not. It's just that ... that blackout seemed awfully suspicious, didn't it?"

His grin widened. "I knew you wouldn't be able to resist."

I smacked him on the arm. It was like hitting a block of stone. Those biceps were *solid*.

"I'm sure everyone in the room thought the same thing. If it was a coincidence, it was awfully convenient for the thief."

He cocked his head to one side. "You never know. It might have been a crime of opportunity—the lights went out, and someone took advantage of the moment."

I frowned at him. "You don't really believe that."

"No," he admitted. "I'd say someone flicked the circuit-breaker that controlled the lights in the ballroom."

"How do you know?"

"Because the fuse box was the first thing the kitchen staff checked, and they found the circuit-breaker in the off position."

"But it could have tripped on its own, couldn't it?"

"It might. But it seems unlikely, doesn't it? If there actually was a power overload that tripped the circuit-breaker, someone only had seconds to decide to take advantage of the sudden darkness in the ballroom to pull off the crime. Pretty daring."

I nodded. "And they'd have no idea how long the lights

would stay off for. They could just as easily be caught in the act when they came back on. It seems an odd thing to do on the spur of the moment. Where is the fuse box located?"

"In a hallway between the kitchen and the delivery dock."

"How far is that from the ballroom?"

"Not far. The most direct route is through the kitchen and down a short flight of stairs—where I should probably go right now, in fact." He stroked one large hand down my bare arm, leaving goosebumps in its wake. "I'm sorry."

"Don't be." I smiled up at him. "I'll see you soon."

I was still smiling after him when Aunt Evie appeared. "Curtis is staying?"

"Yes. I think Delia is, too."

"Would you like a lift home, then?"

"Yes, please."

We said goodnight to Priya and Emily, and then to a few more people as we made our way to the head of the stairs. Everyone wanted to talk to Aunt Evie about the missing necklace, and I could see her shoulders tightening with every comment. She was still smiling, but the smile was looking more and more forced. I was glad when we finally made it outside into the warm summer night.

Christmas was only around the corner, and at this time of year it never really cooled down, even in the middle of the night. Aussie Christmases were a far cry from the typical northern hemisphere experience. Even though we decorated with snowmen and reindeer and all the iconic Christmas symbols, we spent Christmas Day enjoying a swim or hiding from the heat in air-conditioned homes. No white Christmases for us.

Aunt Evie flapped the ends of her silk shawl in an effort to cool her hot face. "My goodness, it's so humid tonight. I can't wait to get home to get these stockings off."

"My feet are killing me," I said. "I'm not used to wearing heels anymore."

"You can take them off when we get to the car." She led the way down the path to the carpark, past frangipani trees covered in sweet-scented flowers.

"It was a good night," I said to the back of her head. "Everything ran very smoothly."

"Until the thief struck. That certainly wasn't in the plan."

"No. But the police will find them."

She sighed, a sad, deflated noise that reminded me how old she was. "I hope so, love, but I must say I don't think it's very likely. The necklace is so small. I'm sure someone carried it away in their pocket and we'll never know where it went."

"The police searched everyone," I reminded her as she unlocked her little red convertible.

"Yes, but a little bit of a pat-down is hardly a thorough search, is it?" She turned the key in the ignition, then stared out the windscreen, her hands motionless on the wheel. "It's just such a lot of money. It would have been our best Yule Ball fundraiser ever. And now the hospital will be short. Thirty-two thousand dollars, Charlie. I don't know how the thief can live with themselves."

She sighed again before putting the car into gear and pulling out of her parking spot.

"It's an awful thing to do," I agreed. "Curtis told me that someone probably threw the circuit-breaker switch, so the thief must have had an accomplice. If they can find out who that was, they'll be a lot closer to solving the crime."

"I'd feel a lot better if *you* were on the case," Aunt Evie said. "You have a natural talent for this sort of thing."

"I don't see how you can say that. I've never had anything to do with investigating a theft."

She waved one hand impatiently at me, the diamond of her engagement ring glittering as it caught the light from the streetlights. "You know what I mean. More than once now, you've found clues and made connections that the police just didn't see. Your brain works differently to most people's. It's all sort of ... squirrely."

I choked on a laugh. "Squirrely? You think I'm nuts?"

"*No*. It's busy and quick and ... oh, I don't even know what I'm trying to say anymore. I'm so tired and discouraged. I mean, really, what is the point of doing all that work to organise the ball when some *dirtbag* is just going to waltz in at the end and steal all the fruits of our labour?"

I cast a sharp glance at her. Aunt Evie was such a positive person usually, but she sounded utterly dispirited.

"Do you want me to drive?"

"No, love, I'm fine. I'm just upset. I can't help thinking of the children."

I blinked. If anyone in this car was *squirrely*, Aunt Evie was a far better candidate than I was. "Which children would those be?"

"The ones in the hospital. Jim Van Doolen dresses up as Santa for them every year—you know him, he's on the committee with me—and gives out presents at the hospital on Christmas Eve. He and I usually deliver one of those big fake cheques to the hospital director at the same time, with the proceeds from the ball."

"Christmas Eve isn't far away."

"That's what I mean. If the police don't find the necklace by then, the cheque will be such a disappointment."

"I doubt the kids will care how big the cheque is, as long as they still get presents."

"I suppose so." She chewed her lip, eyes fixed on the road. "If you ask me, the police should be focusing on that boy Patrick."

"Patrick who?"

"McGuffin or McGibbons or something. He was one of the waiters tonight—the skinny boy with the shaved head. He had such lovely red hair, too. Curls that would make an angel weep. But I suppose that didn't look tough enough in jail."

"He was in *jail*?"

"Well, I suppose you'd call it juvie, since he was under eighteen at the time. Had a very wild youth, that boy."

I vaguely recalled a waiter with a shaven head. He'd had very fair skin. I remembered thinking that with such fair eyebrows, he probably shouldn't have shaved his head, because he looked like an egg.

Aunt Evie's face bore an expression I knew all too well. It was the face of a woman who'd made up her mind, and I had learned over the years that it was very difficult to talk her out of something once she'd set her mind to it.

"And you're assuming that it was him because he already has a criminal record?"

"It stands to reason, doesn't it? And he was collecting plates from Geraldine's table when she got up to get on the stage, so he was close enough." She nodded decisively. "If the police had checked *his* pockets more thoroughly, we'd be having a very different conversation right now. A leopard doesn't change its spots."

"What about presumption of innocence?"

"That boy doesn't even know how to *spell* the word."

"Presumably the Metropole wouldn't employ him if they thought he was likely to steal again. He might have learned his lesson, you know."

"You sound just like Amina."

I blinked. "What's Amina got to do with anything?"

"She gave him a job when he first came out of prison, as a receptionist at her surgery. She said someone that young deserved a chance to show that they'd been rehabilitated and were ready to rejoin society."

"And then what happened? She sacked him?"

"No, he still works there part-time. Always wears a tie to work, very polite. Butter wouldn't melt, to look at him.

The waiting job is just an occasional thing, as far as I know. She said he's studying part-time, too."

"Sounds like a model citizen. Maybe he's turned over a new leaf."

"And maybe he saw his chance tonight when the lights went out," she said tartly as she pulled up outside my house. "Old habits die hard, you know. And now his profit is the hospital's loss."

She looked so frazzled that I laid a hand on her arm. "The police know all about his record. If it was him, I'm sure they'll be all over it. You'll have the necklace back in no time."

"I wish I could believe that. I don't know how I'll ever get to sleep tonight." She shook her head. "The stress, you know."

She laid a hand on her heart, as if she could feel the stress building in her chest at that very moment. I narrowed my eyes. I could smell a performance coming on.

"And at my age, stress is a killer," she added.

"Aunt Evie."

"I could have a heart attack."

"*Aunt Evie.*"

"If only I had a clever niece who could help."

"You are shameless."

"If you won't do it for me, think of the children."

I snorted. "Absolutely *shameless*. Fine, fine. I'll talk to Amina, I guess, and find out what she knows about him."

"Thank you, darling."

I opened the door and got out of the car. "I can't

believe, after I spent all night avoiding Amina, now I have to go talk to her."

Aunt Evie smiled sweetly, pleased now that she'd rail-roaded me into agreeing to investigate. "She'll probably give you the third degree about that neighbour of yours, too. Have fun, darling!"

CHAPTER 6

THE NEXT MORNING, I WAS WOKEN BY A COLD, WET NOSE THRUST abruptly into my face. Though I loved the owner of said nose very much, I wouldn't recommend it as a method for waking up.

"Rufus, get off!" He was standing right next to the bed, his face on my pillow. I gave him a shove, but he took it as an invitation to lick my hand. "What time is it?"

In my defence, it had been a late night and I was still pretty groggy, otherwise it wouldn't have taken me so long to realise that there wasn't a lot of point asking a golden retriever to tell me the time. He was a smart dog, but he wasn't *that* smart.

After some effort, my bleary eyes focused on my Fitbit and I discovered it was almost half past eight. That explained the damp wake-up call. Rufus was used to an earlier start.

"Are you hungry, boy? Do you want some breakfast?"

He wagged enthusiastically. *Breakfast* was one of the

words he recognised, along with *dinner, walk, ball,* and *what on earth is that in your mouth?* (He usually took off in the opposite direction when I said that one.)

"Okay, give me a minute."

He huffed his hot, doggy breath into my face, which encouraged me to move a little faster. Fifteen minutes later I was downstairs, showered, dressed, and ready to dispense kibble-shaped largesse to any deserving dogs in the vicinity. I let him out for a quick wee, then he bolted back inside to sit patiently by his bowl just to prove what a deserving dog he was. His previous owner, Bert, had trained him well, and even though he'd had some time with Bert's widow, who quite frankly had rather neglected him, he was quickly remembering his training now he was with me.

After that, I downed a bowl of cereal while Rufus gallivanted around the yard, checking it for suspicious nocturnal activity. You just never knew when the neighbourhood cats or possums would invade, necessitating much sniffing and weeing over their scents. When we were both ready, we headed off to the shops together. It was a beautiful sunny morning, which would probably turn stinking hot later, so it was a good chance to get in a walk before the outside temperature became unbearable.

Rufus stopped at the top of the wooden stairs that led down to the beach and looked back at me enquiringly.

"Not today, boy." If I let him onto the beach, he'd end up wet and covered in sand. Most of the shopkeepers in Sunny Bay were relaxed about Rufus visiting, but only if he wasn't likely to stink up their shop with the smell of wet dog. "I've got to finish my Christmas shopping today."

He gave me a reproachful look that suggested that Christmas shopping was nowhere near as important as giving a dog a good run on the beach.

"You think that now," I told him, "but you're going to love your present. Just wait until Christmas Day."

Normally, I didn't give many presents. Last year I'd only bought something for Aunt Evie, my scumbag ex Will, and my equally scummy ex-best friend Amy and her little daughter. But this year I felt like celebrating my new life and all the lovely people in it, so I'd bought a book for each of the book club ladies, and the most gorgeous earrings for Aunt Evie. They were huge and coloured like peacock feathers—just the kind of thing she loved. I didn't know Curtis well enough yet to come up with anything amazing for him, so I thought I'd get him a movie voucher. Everyone liked going to the movies, right?

I had toy cars for Heidi's twins, a bottle of wine for my neighbour Jack, *several* dog toys and the most enormous bone in the freezer for Rufus—but I still needed something for Curtis's daughter Maisie. Because when all was said and done, Christmas is really about the kids, and she was absolutely my favourite kid right now. One of my favourite people, full stop, in fact. It made buying her something a little more challenging, as I wanted it to be as special as she was.

We were walking past Denise's flower shop when I spotted Priya's mum coming out of the newsagent. Without even thinking, I leapt into the doorway of the florist to hide. Priya's fake relationship with Jack had me that spooked.

Rufus thought we were playing a game and charged into the shop, almost knocking over a bucket full of roses on the floor.

"Rufus, no!" I shouted, lunging for his collar to drag him away.

I hadn't put him on a lead, since he was normally so well-behaved on our walks. He gave me a disappointed look and followed me out again, while I apologised to Denise and steadied a couple of roses that looked about ready to take a swan dive onto the floor.

Our little commotion had alerted Amina to our presence, and she was rapidly bearing down on us with all the determination of a galleon under full sail. *Ready the guns. Aye, aye, captain.* I pasted a smile on my face, remembering belatedly that I actually wanted to talk to her about her employee Patrick. Maybe if I played my cards right I could divert her from her obsession with finding out every last detail about her daughter's supposed new boyfriend.

"Hello, Charlie," she said. "Is that your dog?"

"Yes. This is Rufus."

"Should you be walking him without a lead?"

"He's very well trained," I said.

She gave me a doubtful look, no doubt recalling my desperate dive after him a moment earlier. "How does your neighbour feel about having such a big dog next door? You did say he liked animals, didn't you?"

You had to hand it to her—she could turn any conversation into an opportunity to grill me on the subject of Jack.

"He's very fond of Rufus," I said. As far as I could tell, Jack was perfectly happy having *a big dog* like Rufus next door. His cat, Sherlock, may not have felt the same, but since Sherlock was old and rarely ventured outside, it hadn't been a problem.

"Priya didn't tell me anything about him," she said.

I was confused until I realised she meant about Jack, not about Rufus.

"It's, um, a very new relationship," I offered lamely.

Man, I hated lying to Amina, even to help Priya. Plus, I was a terrible liar, and I could feel a blush crawling up my neck and into my cheeks. Any minute now, Amina would realise I was telling porkies and the game would be up.

"When did they meet?" she asked. "How serious do you think it is?"

She asked how serious it was as if she were asking about a cancer diagnosis. *Is it Stage Four? Has it gone to the heart yet?* This was one mama who wasn't happy with her daughter's choices.

"I ... ah." I flailed around, getting more uncomfortable by the minute. "I couldn't say. You'd have to ask them. You're seeing them on Saturday night, right?"

Amina's eyes had a sad, faraway look. "It's so unlike Priya to keep things from me."

"I'm sure she didn't mean to," I said hurriedly, unhappily aware of the real hurt in her eyes.

"We used to be so close."

I shifted uneasily, wishing that Priya had found some

other way to solve her problem with her mother. What would happen when Amina found out it was all a sham? Priya was so confident she could pull it off, but I was in Aunt Evie's camp on this one. These kind of secrets had a way of coming out.

"I'm sure you'll love Jack," I said as cheerily as I could manage, then quickly changed the subject. "Have you recovered from all the excitement last night?"

"It *was* a more eventful night than we expected," she said, momentarily diverted from the Priya conversation.

"Poor Aunt Evie's very upset about it," I said.

Amina nodded. "I imagine so. The loss of the necklace leaves a big hole. Such a shame that the hospital won't be getting that equipment they want for the children's ward after all. Do you know if the police have any leads?"

"Ah ... there was some talk about a waiter called Patrick." It was true—there had been some talk, just by Aunt Evie, not the police. But I had promised to find out what I could about him from Amina.

Her brows drew together in a frown. "Patrick McGuigan? It's shameful how the police treat him."

"Doesn't he have a criminal record?"

"A *juvenile* record," she corrected, treating me to a glare cold enough to turn me into a popsicle. "For which he has done time, and it shouldn't be continually thrown in his face."

Wow, all of a sudden I had a new appreciation for Priya's determination not to cause drama with her mother. Angry Amina was fearsome. I bent down to pat Rufus's silky head, just to have an excuse to break eye contact, though I fancied I could still feel her glare boring into the top of my head.

"So you don't think he'd do something like that?"

"Not at all. He works three days a week as a receptionist for us, and you couldn't hope to find a nicer young man. All our older patients love him. He regularly handles money at the surgery and I have complete faith in him. He truly has changed, you know. He and his girlfriend are expecting a baby in the new year."

Not that impending fatherhood was proof of a good character, but I nodded. It seemed safest. Rufus sat down and leaned heavily against my leg.

"The police searched him last night, you know. *And* his locker at the hotel. Very thoroughly, from what he told me. But you know what gossip is like in a town like this. I'm sure everyone is already convinced he's guilty. Whatever happened to presumption of innocence?" She threw her neatly manicured hands up in a gesture of outrage, frowning at me as if I, personally, was leading the charge with torch and pitchfork to convict her innocent receptionist.

"Then I'm sure he has nothing to worry about," I said. "The truth will come out. Well, I'd love to chat." *Lies.* "But I guess I'd better not hold you up any longer. And I have Christmas shopping to do."

I nudged Rufus with my knee and he stood up, giving me a long-suffering look, as if to say *but I just got comfortable.*

She nodded, unsmiling. "I'll see you later."

Well, on the bright side, she didn't seem interested in

interrogating me any further about Jack. On the not-so-bright side, I now felt like a heel and Amina was barely talking to me.

"Come on, Rufus," I said.

He glanced up at me, then licked my knee thoughtfully as we set off. At least *he* still liked me.

CHAPTER 7

THE BELL OVER THE DOOR OF TOY STORIES TINKLED CHEERFULLY as I entered, having persuaded Rufus to wait outside. Heidi wasn't immediately visible. In fact, the shop seemed surprisingly quiet considering this was her busiest time of year.

"Hello?" I called, pausing at the counter.

The place was a Christmas explosion. Tinsel hung from the ceiling and festooned the counter and the cash register. A small, waist-high Christmas tree loaded with shiny baubles stood in a corner of the picture book area, where usually a squishy blue beanbag sat. Presents that I assumed were only empty boxes wrapped in festive paper were piled underneath the tree, and a giant inflatable Santa swayed in the front window.

"Coming!" Heidi's voice called from the depths of the shop, shortly followed by Heidi herself.

As she often did, she wore her hair in two plaited pigtails, but today they were twined with silver tinsel. A happy reindeer with a big red nose adorned her T-shirt, and she was wearing red shorts and sparkly red sneakers to complete the look. A pair of silver Christmas trees dangled from her earlobes.

"Oh, hi, Charlie! How are you?"

"I'm good, thanks. You're looking very festive."

She grinned. "The kids love it. I've got three Christmas T-shirts and I wear a different one every day."

Her grin was infectious—I couldn't resist the dimple that peeked out when she was really amused. Apparently I had a thing for dimples, though Curtis's had a much different effect on me than Heidi's did.

"Are you sure it's only the kids who love it?" I glanced around the shop. "You're really getting into the Christmas spirit here."

"Christmas is my favourite time of the year. The little ones get so excited. I just love seeing their faces light up when they come in."

That didn't surprise me at all. Heidi had a real knack for connecting with kids that sprang from her genuine interest in small people. If she hadn't found her calling in running a children's book and toy store, she would have made a great kindergarten teacher.

"Are you shopping today or just dropping in?" she asked.

"Shopping, actually. I want to get something for Maisie, but I'm not sure what six-year-old girls are into these days. It's been a while since I was six, and I'm sure things have changed."

"Well, you've come to the right place," she said. "Six-year-olds are my specialty."

"The boys are only five, aren't they?" I asked, referring to her twins, Noah and Zach.

"Five years and three-quarters, actually, as Zach keeps reminding me. Practically six, Noah says. Their birthday's in February and they have a countdown calendar in their bedroom. Noah is keeping a running list of all the things he thinks we should get him for his birthday."

"I didn't realise turning six was such a big deal."

"It's the presents they care about, more than the age. Zach says I should have made their birthday in the middle of the year so their presents were more evenly spread. He's always complaining that he has to wait *all year* to get any presents, and then he gets two lots close together and it's all over again for another year. He's been trying to convince me that they deserve extra because of that." She smiled fondly. "Dave says he'll make a great lawyer one day."

I laughed. "Tell Dave not to hope for a lawyer. He'd be better off with a son with more practical skills, like a plumber or something."

"Or maybe an IT guy. Then he could look after my website." She glanced over my shoulder towards the door. "Oh, is that Rufus outside? Let me get him something."

She dived behind the counter and came out with a small rawhide treat.

"You don't have to do that," I said as she headed for the door.

"But he's being such a good boy—look at him sitting

there so patiently!" She opened the door and crooned to him in that baby voice that dog lovers all seem to use.

He wagged happily and was only too eager to accept his treat, chomping down on it with gusto.

"You know he'll expect something every time he comes here now," I said as she shut the door again.

She grinned, showing a complete lack of concern. "Did you have any idea what you'd like for Maisie?"

"Maybe a book? But not just any old book. Something special."

She led me over to the bookshelves. "A special book for a special little girl? How about this one?"

She showed me a few with beautiful illustrations, and I eventually settled on a gorgeous book of fairy tales.

"What about her dad?" Heidi asked with a teasing smile. "Have you got something special for him, too?"

I eyed her suspiciously, trying to figure out if that was innuendo or not. "I'm getting movie vouchers. I didn't know what else to get."

"Hmmm. Yeah, I guess he's already got handcuffs. You know, I saw a pink fluffy pair last time I was down in Newcastle."

Definitely innuendo.

"I don't think pink's his colour. And I don't want to know what kind of shops you've been frequenting in Newcastle."

She laughed. "Well, movie vouchers will be nice. Make sure you sit in the back row!"

I rolled my eyes. Time to change the subject before I started blushing.

"I ran into Amina just now. I don't think I'm her favourite person anymore."

"Oh? Why? Did you tell her Jack's a serial killer?"

"No. I suggested her receptionist might be the person who stole the necklace at the Yule Ball."

"Candace Bradshaw?" Her eyes widened in shock.

"No. The part-time guy. Patrick McGuigan. He was working as a waiter at the ball."

"The one with the shaved head?"

"That's him." I quickly filled her in on what Amina had told me about him.

"Sounds like the police have been all over him already."

"Yes. I mean, he might have managed to sneak it out somehow, but it doesn't seem very likely."

"Besides, he must have known, with his record, that he'd be the first person they'd look at." Her eyes got a distant look to them. "If I remember right, he got into trouble as a teen for breaking into the school and smashing things up. Did it more than once, because he had an issue with the principal. He even set fire to the library one year in the Christmas holidays."

"So he wasn't a thief?"

"Well, he might have stolen the odd thing, too, but it was more vandalism."

"But just at the school?"

"Yes."

I didn't know whether to feel relieved or disappointed. "Doesn't sound like he's our thief, then."

"No, it doesn't." She stopped to greet a customer and

direct them to the Lego section of the store, then turned back to me. "So who else have you got? You *are* investigating it, right?"

I shrugged one shoulder awkwardly. "I'm sure the police will sort it out, but I kind of promised Aunt Evie that I'd look into a few things. She's so upset about it."

Heidi nodded. "I can understand that. Evie puts so much work into that ball every year."

"And I did see one odd thing."

Her eyes sparked with interest. "Ooh, what? Tell me!"

"Do you know Geraldine Winderbaum's daughter?"

"Flick? Of course."

"Flick is such a weird name."

"It's short for Felicity, but no one ever calls her that."

"What's her last name?"

"She's a Winderbaum, too. Irving adopted her when she was a kid. I think she was only a baby when Geraldine and her dad divorced, and then husband number three didn't last long, so Irving's been around most of her life. What about her?"

"Well, after the ball was over, I was chatting outside the ballroom with Emily and Priya and I saw Flick talking to this new bartender called Tim."

She rang up my purchase and placed the beautiful book in a bag almost tenderly. "And?"

"And I saw him give her something small. It was too small for me to see what it was—"

"But it might have been a necklace?"

I shrugged and handed over my credit card. "Maybe.

That doesn't seem right, though, does it? If she's got it, why haven't they called off the police search?"

She frowned thoughtfully. "Didn't Evie say at the last book club meeting that Flick wasn't happy with her mother for donating that necklace?"

It was my turn to frown. "I don't remember that."

She waved a hand airily. "You were probably too focused on solving crimes to be paying attention. It was just a throwaway comment when we were having tea afterwards. Something about how the necklace had been given to Geraldine by Flick's dad, so Flick thought she should inherit it."

"She and Geraldine did seem to be having some kind of spat," I said, remembering the frown on Geraldine's face as she berated her daughter after Tim had left. She'd had a lot to say about something that Flick hadn't been very receptive to, judging by the mutinous look on her face. Was it possible that Flick had arranged for someone to steal her own mother's necklace rather than lose it in an auction? "But why would she go to all the trouble of having someone steal it for her at the ball when she could have taken it from her mother herself? I assume she'd have keys to her mother's house."

"I think she still lives there, actually."

"Even easier, then."

Heidi shrugged. "There was a whole ballroom full of suspects at the ball. Maybe she thought that would take suspicion away from her."

"She could have just faked a break-in," I said.

"True. And I don't see how she could really enjoy the

necklace—it's not as though she could wear it in public when everyone knows it's been stolen. Imagine if Geraldine saw it!"

I accepted my package from Heidi distractedly, mind still busy with the problem. "Maybe just possessing it is enough. But if Tim *had* stolen the necklace at the ball and given it to Flick outside, shouldn't she have been happier about it? She looked kind of shocked about whatever he passed to her."

I lowered my voice at the end, since the customer who'd been looking for Lego was approaching the counter with a gigantic, colourful box in her arms.

"I guess that's something you'll have to figure out," Heidi said. "Good luck!"

She gave me a little wave as she turned to the woman and I headed outside. Rufus had finished his treat. Knowing him, he'd probably finished it within three seconds of receiving it. He wagged happily at seeing me, though he was a good boy and didn't leave the sit position until I told him "okay".

He sniffed a little doubtfully at my book bag.

"It's a present for Maisie," I told him. "A book of fairy tales with the most gorgeous illustrations, plus a dragon on the cover. You can't go wrong with a dragon on the cover, boy."

He licked my hand thoughtfully, which I took to be agreement.

CHAPTER 8

I WAS STILL DISCUSSING IT WITH RUFUS THAT AFTERNOON. IF anyone had heard me they probably would have thought I was crazy, talking to a dog as though I expected him to join the conversation, but the truth was, speaking aloud helped me to work through things.

Plus, Rufus seemed to enjoy being included.

"So if it's not Patrick, who's our thief?" I was sitting on the lounge with my feet up on the coffee table, my laptop competing for space in my lap with Rufus's head. He was sprawled on the lounge beside me, getting his long golden hairs over everything, but I didn't care. I liked the company, and the lounge was beige, so they didn't show up too badly.

I'd been mulling over this question ever since I got home from the shops and all through lunch. I had to admit, Flick was starting to look suspicious.

"If Heidi's right that she didn't want that necklace

given away, she has a motive," I pointed out to Rufus. "I'll have to check with Aunt Evie."

I picked up my phone and dialled. Rufus sighed, his hot breath huffing across my bare leg, and resettled his head more comfortably. I shifted the laptop slightly to give him more room, since his nose was practically touching the space bar.

"Just a quick question," I said when Aunt Evie answered.

"Yes?"

"Heidi told me that Flick wasn't happy about Geraldine donating that necklace. Is that true?"

"Apparently, she'd always assumed she'd inherit it, since her father gave it to Geraldine, but she must have gotten over it. Geraldine wouldn't have donated it otherwise, would she?"

I wasn't so sure about that. Geraldine didn't strike me as the kind of person to care much about other people's desires.

"So, maybe she *hasn't* gotten over it. Maybe she's the one who stole it—except that makes me wonder why she'd choose to steal it in such a risky way in a public place, instead of taking it at home."

"That's easy," Aunt Evie said. "She doesn't have the combination to her mother's safe."

"You think so? I bet Geraldine's got it written down somewhere so she doesn't forget it."

Ladies of that generation weren't as good on things like password—or safe combination—security as younger people. Case in point: Aunt Evie carefully copied the combination for her own safe into the back of her new diary every year.

"I bet she hasn't. Geraldine's had four husbands, and three divorces have left her a little paranoid. She likes to be sure she has a stash of money and jewels that's out of everyone's reach except hers. I'm telling you, no one has that combination except her. Not even Irving."

"Wow." I digested that for a moment. "How do you *know* this stuff?"

"She told me so herself. She's quite proud of the fact. Says she's not going to be caught out again."

"Well, it seems quite understanding of Irving."

Aunt Evie laughed. "Oh, don't worry, Irving's just as bad. He made her sign a pre-nup before they got married."

Pre-nuptial agreements didn't work as well in Australia as they did in other countries, due to our legislation around divorce and family settlements, but full marks to Irving for trying.

"So, maybe the ball *was* Flick's only chance to grab the necklace. Interesting."

"So, does this mean that you don't think Patrick did it?" She sounded a little disappointed to let go of her theory.

"No. To hear Amina tell it, the guy's a saint. I'm looking into other possibilities."

"Such as Flick."

"Such as Flick," I agreed. "Anyway, I'll get back to it. Talk to you soon."

I'd decided to go through my photos of the night, particularly the ones I'd snapped immediately after the lights came back on. Looking at the photos of an event had helped me crack the case before, and I was hoping to at least be able to rule some people in or out, depending on where they were in the room in the seconds after the robbery.

"Maybe Flick's the one who turned out the lights, and Tim snatched it for her," I said to Rufus. "Do you think she paid him? Or maybe they're old friends."

Rufus's eyebrows twitched, but that was the only sign that he heard me. I clicked to the next photo and saw my theory go up in flames. Flick and Tim were both in the shot. Flick was standing chatting to someone at the next table. Tim was just behind Aunt Evie, with a stack of beer glasses cradled carefully against one arm, looking up at the lights with a quizzical expression. Both of them were too far from an exit to have turned off the lights somewhere down the corridor to the kitchen and have made it back in time before they came on again.

"Okay, so maybe Tim really was giving her an earring she'd dropped and he has nothing to do with the crime." Although there was that shocked look Flick had given him when he handed the supposed earring over. Never mind, I could think about that later. "Could Flick have made it to the stage and back to here before the lights came on? I'd have to say yes, so she could still be our thief." I jiggled my leg, bouncing Rufus's head up and down. "You know, I'm doing my best detecting here. You could at least pretend to be interested."

Tim was also close enough to the stage to have snatched the necklace, assuming I could come up with a reason for him to be doing Flick's dirty work. It was a bit of a stretch, considering how many glasses he was juggling, but you never knew. He still had one hand free.

Judging by how many glasses were teetering in his stack, he was on his way back to the bar when the lights came on. If he'd detoured to nab the necklace, he could have hidden it in his pocket, then whisked it away out of sight behind the bar somewhere before anyone even realised that it was gone. Possible, but not probable, unless he had some A-grade juggling skills.

Amina's receptionist, Patrick of the chequered past, was in this image too. Aunt Evie thought he'd been right by Geraldine's table, but he'd moved on. It just went to show you that eye witnesses could be unreliable. In fact, he was in the middle of the room, loaded up with dirty plates to be taken to the kitchen. Considering the size of the ballroom, it seemed highly improbable that he could have put them down, threaded his way through the tables to the front, stolen the necklace, and made his way back again without falling over something or being caught in the act. I'd have to give this photo to the police so they could stop harassing him.

"That would make Amina happy," I told Rufus.

He sighed, then wriggled furiously until he was on his back, his head still pillowed in my lap. His tail thumped against a throw pillow.

"Is that your way of suggesting you'd like a tummy rub?" I obliged, of course. He was simply irresistible. "You're not being any help at all here, you know that? And here I am trying to find a missing necklace and save

Christmas for the hospital. So what do you think? Flick or Tim? Or both?"

Really the only reason I had to suspect either of them was that weird moment afterwards, when Tim passed something to her and she'd looked so shocked. Well, that and the fact that she'd wasted no time shoving it into her purse to hide it from her mother.

Geraldine hadn't seemed at all happy to find them together. Surely there had to be something peculiar going on? If Tim truly had been returning a dropped earring, why had Geraldine's face looked like a thundercloud? And what had she been so furiously whispering to Flick after Tim had made his escape?

He'd denied knowing Flick when I'd asked, but I didn't believe him. There had to be some history there to make Geraldine storm over the minute she saw them together. So why had he lied?

I needed to find out how Flick knew the new bartender in town and what their relationship was. Something wasn't adding up.

CHAPTER 9

THAT NIGHT, I WAS EATING A QUICK DINNER AFTER AN afternoon photo shoot with a local family wanting Christmas pictures for their Christmas card. They'd left it a bit late, considering that Christmas was about ten days away, but I wasn't complaining. More photo shoots meant more money in my own Christmas kitty, and besides, they'd had the three cutest little girls. Shoots involving kids were always harder, and the more kids in the mix the more challenging it became. But it was so very rewarding when you got that one perfect shot where all three looked like little angels in their Christmas best. Their mum was going to be *so* happy when she saw the photos.

And I was discovering that making people happy was my jam. I couldn't have predicted how much more fun running a photography business was than working in corporate HR, but I didn't have a single regret about my change in career. Or about my change in location. Life in Sunrise Bay was better than I'd ever dreamed.

My phone chimed with a new text coming in. Speaking of dreams come true, it was Curtis.

Sorry again about last night. Can I make it up to you with dinner on Saturday?

Sure! I'd love that. Not that you have anything to be sorry for.

Great. Pick you up around 7? Where do you want to go?

Honestly, I didn't care where we went, as long as I got to spend time with Curtis. But Priya had told me about a new Thai restaurant in Waterloo Bay, so I suggested it.

After a bit more chatting, I asked him how the investigation into the theft of the necklace was going. He didn't reply straight away, and I wondered if he was going to give me the usual police line about not divulging details of ongoing investigations.

Been making enquiries, but I reckon it's long gone.

Really? That was bad news for Aunt Evie.

Jewellery easy to move. Can break it up, reset stones.

And no one would ever know.

Right. Best chance of finding it was on the night.

I grimaced as I put the phone down and scooped up another mouthful of spaghetti bolognaise. That meant my chance of success was pretty low, too.

Well, all I could do was try.

Gotta go, I texted as I finished my dinner. *Meeting Priya for drinks.*

Have fun, he texted back.

I grinned as I grabbed my handbag and gave Rufus a goodbye pat. I had no head for alcohol, so I'd probably only have one drink, but having fun was a given. Priya always made me laugh, even if sometimes she made me shake my head at the same time.

She waved madly as I entered the bar at the Metropole. She already had a table, with three cocktails at the ready. I made my way through the room, which was only half full, nodding to a couple of people I knew.

"Three drinks?" I asked. "Who else is coming?"

"Jack said he was going to drop in so we could get our stories straight for the big night on Saturday." Her tone was casual. Too casual?

I cocked my head at her as I took a seat. "You've been seeing Jack?"

"Just texting."

I nodded, smiling, and she added, "It's not like that."

"Like what?"

"Whatever you're thinking in that devious brain of yours. Swapping numbers is no big deal. How else are we going to coordinate Operation Hoodwink?"

"I wasn't thinking anything," I protested. "And I do not have a devious brain."

"Oh, yeah? I suppose that's why you're investigating this jewellery theft. Because you're so terrible at deducing things from miniscule clues."

I picked up my drink, which was a murky brown colour and smelled strongly of rum. "Let's not talk about that. Curtis just told me that he doesn't think we'll ever find it, so now I'm feeling all gloomy about breaking the news to Aunt Evie."

"Better drown your sorrows, then." She lifted her own drink in salute. "Cheers."

I took a sip and burst out coughing. Priya laughed as my eyes watered.

"What on earth is *in* this?" I asked when I'd recovered enough to speak.

"Vodka, rum, tequila, and a few other goodies."

I gazed at the glass in astonishment. "Good heavens. That's a drink-driving charge in a glass."

"You'll be fine," she said. "Plenty of time before you have to get back behind the wheel. Live a little."

I took a more cautious sip of my drink and managed not to splutter this time. "I'm not sure that burning a hole in my oesophagus counts as *living a little*."

Priya waved an airy hand. "Stick with me, kid, you'll get to experience all life's highs and lows. How's work?"

I told her about my most recent photo shoot and we chatted for a while about inconsequential things. I did notice, however, that her eyes strayed towards the door more than once, and I hid a smile behind my glass.

Was Priya actually interested in Jack? He certainly seemed interested in her—what man in his right mind would agree to such a deception if he didn't fancy the woman? But Priya had seemed oblivious. Maybe that was just a cover. I resolved to watch them both carefully for any signs of budding romance.

I didn't have to wait long for my chance. Jack breezed in, still in his scrubs, and dumped his backpack on the spare seat at our table.

"And how's my fabulous girlfriend tonight?" he asked as he flopped into a seat and lifted the waiting drink to his lips.

"Fabulous as ever," Priya replied, lifting her glass in a toast.

"What about me?" I demanded. "You don't care about your beloved neighbour anymore now you've hooked up with the town hottie?"

He laughed. "Of course I do. How is my beloved neighbour?"

"Stressed about this scheme you two have cooked up. How am I ever going to look Amina in the face again?"

He held both hands up, palms out. "Stop right there. I had no hand in cooking this up. That was all Priya."

"You were just crazy enough to say yes."

"Guilty as charged."

"You worry too much," Priya said. "It will be fine. Mum will be satisfied once she's met him, and then we can all go back to normal. And I won't have her trying to micro-manage my love life anymore."

If she thought that, she didn't know her own mother very well. Amina struck me as the type to love nothing more than a good bit of micromanaging, and I very much doubted she'd be put off by the sudden appearance of a "boyfriend". Especially one who might not meet her exacting criteria.

Priya grinned at Jack. "I must say, it's very thoughtful of you to be a shift worker. It's the perfect excuse for why you'll never turn up to another family function again."

Jack looked down at his drink, one finger idly rubbing a line through the condensation on the glass. "Well, if you need me to ... I could always do it again. You know, if your mother gets too demanding."

There was a short silence while they both gazed fixedly at their drinks and I cast around for an excuse to exit the conversation. I'd never seen a more awkward flirtation in my life.

"Oh, look, there's Emily!" I could barely hide the relief in my voice when I spotted my friend at the bar. "I'll just go over and say hello."

Maybe Priya and Jack would have sorted themselves out by the time I got back. If anything was ever going to bloom between them, they probably needed some privacy anyway.

"Hi, Em!" I slid onto the barstool next to hers. "How's things?"

"Oh, hi. Not bad. It's Friday tomorrow, so that always helps."

"You look gorgeous. Are you meeting someone?"

She was wearing a sleeveless sheath dress in a rich red that set off her dark hair and eyes. She lifted one delicate shoulder and eyed me from under the long fall of her hair. "I thought Tim was working tonight. That's what he told me at the ball."

Right. I'd been too busy thinking about the theft but I remembered now that Emily had mentioned that. I glanced over at the bartender automatically—a girl with flame-red hair and a diamond stud in her nose. Definitely not Tim.

"Maybe he's coming in later."

"Nope." Emily took a sip of her wine and nodded at the bartender. "I already asked. She doesn't know when his next shift is either. Guess I got all dressed up for nothing."

"Do you want to join us?" I gestured at the table where Priya and Jack were chatting. They looked more comfortable together now. If the awkward moment was past, it might be safe to rejoin them.

Emily's gaze roved over the room, as if she was still searching in vain for her good-looking bartender. "I'll come and say hi, but I might just head home after that. I've got a big day at work tomorrow."

"He wouldn't have left town again, would he?" I looked around the room, too, and spotted Greta, the event coordinator Aunt Evie had introduced me to at the ball. "Didn't he tell you he was travelling around the country?"

"But he'd only just arrived." She looked despondent. "Maybe Greta knows."

Greta was heading towards the bar, and Emily called her over.

"You know her?" I asked.

"I helped out a lot with the Yule Ball last year. Hi, Greta, how are you?"

Greta ordered a chardonnay and slumped onto the stool on Emily's other side. "I've been better. I feel so bad about the Yule Ball."

"It wasn't your fault," I said.

"I know, but poor Evie."

Emily was waiting impatiently to get a word in. "Do you know that new bartender, Tim?"

"The Chinese guy?"

"Yeah. What's he like?"

Greta's drink arrived and she took a sip. "I haven't had much to do with him, but he seems nice enough. Excellent bartender, too. You should see him mix a cocktail—it's a real show."

"How long has he been working here?" I asked.

"Two weeks? Three? I'm not sure. Why the sudden interest?"

"He's kind of cute," Emily said. "I was hoping to see him here tonight. Do you know if he's single?"

"No idea. You'd have to ask him." She grinned. "But I'd advise getting in quickly. I suspect he won't be single for long, with a face like that."

"All the cute guys are taken," Emily muttered as she finished her drink.

"So how is Evie?" Greta asked me when Emily had wandered over to say hello to Priya and Jack.

"She's fine. A little disappointed, but still hoping the police will be able to find the necklace." I didn't tell her that Aunt Evie had asked me to take part in the search, but something occurred to me, now that I had Greta alone.

Curtis had said he didn't think the person who had turned off the lights could have made it back to the ballroom by the time they came back on, because of how far away the fuse box was, but I was keen to see for myself. I just needed an excuse to get into the kitchen and behind the scenes at the hotel.

"While I've got you, can I ask you something?"

"Sure."

"I'm photographing a wedding here in February. I was wondering if I could have a tour of the place before then so I can get a feel for it and work out where I can get the best shots."

"Sure. Let's set something up for January, after the Christmas rush is over."

I chewed my lip. "Actually, I was hoping to squeeze it in before Christmas. I might be going away in January." That wasn't one hundred per cent a lie. I *might* be going away in January, you never knew, though I didn't currently have any plans.

"Which wedding is it?"

"The Mayberry one."

"Oh." She considered for a moment. "Well, if you don't mind a very quick gallop through, I could take you tomorrow. We're setting up for a corporate Christmas party in the smaller function room, which is where they're getting married. We have a lovely spot in the gardens that's perfect for wedding photos. Shall we say around midday? I can't spare much time, I'm sorry."

"Midday will be great. Thank you! I really appreciate it."

"No problem. I'll see you tomorrow."

I headed back to my table, feeling only slightly guilty. I didn't have the police's advantages, so I had to make use of whatever connections I could. If I'd known Greta a little better I would have come right out and told her the real reason I wanted the tour. She seemed lovely, but she might have been one of those people who frowned on amateurs messing around in police investigations, so it was safer this way.

Besides, Greta would be so thrilled if I did manage to locate the missing necklace that she wouldn't mind spending a few minutes taking me on a tour that had nothing to do with photographing a wedding.

CHAPTER 10

I WAS THERE IN PLENTY OF TIME THE NEXT DAY FOR MY TOUR with Greta.

"I think it's going to rain," she said, "so let's look at the garden first, shall we?"

"Sure." I followed her down a quiet, carpeted hallway from the foyer and out a set of double doors that led to a wide terrace paved in warm golden sandstone. The guest car park was to the left, and to the right was a shaded lawn.

"This is where we'll have the wedding ceremony, weather permitting," Greta said, waving a hand at the terrace.

"It's nice." Huge planters were set at intervals along the edge, ferns spilling out of them. "Very green."

Greta gestured at one end of the terrace. "We usually set up a floral arch at that end, and create an aisle from that door down the centre, with chairs set up on either side. It's lovely."

"And if it rains?"

"Not so nice, unfortunately. We have a meeting room that we can use, but there's only room for a few chairs. Everyone else has to stand."

"You can't do it in the function room?"

"Not when all the tables have already been set for the reception. There's not enough floor space. Fingers crossed it'll be a fine day."

I nodded. February was when school went back, and I had many memories of hot, sweltering days that ended in thunderstorms at three o'clock when school got out.

I walked to the edge of the terrace and checked out the grassed area below. A winding path led through the trees and there was a pretty arched bridge over a small artificial pond.

"That looks like a good spot for some wedding photos."

Greta nodded. "A lot of our brides use it. The photos always look lovely. Let me show you the function room—it's just through here."

The function room opened directly off the terrace. It was a large, square room which currently had very little furniture in it. Smaller tables had been put together in a U-shape at one end, facing a large projection screen. The floor was carpeted in a deep blue pattern and a small bar was built into one corner. Opposite the bar was a pair of swinging doors, which I presumed led to the kitchen.

"It's bigger than I expected when you called it the small function room."

"Well, it's smaller than the ballroom." She smiled. "Anyway, it looks a lot smaller when it's set up for a wedding. Sometimes it's so full of tables there's only room for the tiniest dance floor."

I gestured at the double doors. "Is that the kitchen through there?"

"Yes."

"Is there somewhere safe in there where I can leave my camera gear when I'm not using it? I'll be bringing quite a lot of equipment and I don't use it all at once."

"Oh, sure. We have lockers for the staff. There should be a couple free."

"Great. Can I see them? Just to see how much I can fit in," I added when she gave me a puzzled look.

"Sure." She led the way through the doors, which swung shut behind us.

We walked down a long corridor before we arrived at the kitchen itself.

"Is this the same kitchen that services the ballroom?" I asked.

"No, the ballroom has its own separate facility, because it's upstairs. When the ballroom's in use, that's a lot of meals that have to be carted around. Bringing them up and downstairs would make things awkward."

"Are there staff lockers up there, too?"

"No. The lockers are near the staff entry. I'll show you. That's the kitchen in there." She nodded at another set of swing doors as we passed.

Through the windows set into them I could see the

lunchtime cooking was in full swing, and a delicious aroma of cooking meat drifted out. We passed a staircase leading up.

"Does that go to the ballroom?"

"Yes. That's the staff entry. The kitchen's up there."

The corridor opened out into a small foyer of sorts. Lockers stood against one wall, and a sign saying *Staff Toilet* marked a door to one side.

"Here we are," Greta said, opening one of the empty lockers. "How is this? Big enough?"

"That looks great," I said, making a show of inspecting the locker. The key was in the door. "I assume I can just take this key with me?"

"As long as you bring it back," she said with a laugh.

I glanced at the outer door. "Is that unlocked all the time?"

"Pretty much." She opened it to show me a view of the delivery dock. "But don't worry, these lockers are sturdy. Once you've locked it, your gear will be perfectly safe."

That wasn't actually what concerned me. I was thinking how easy it would be for anyone to let themselves in this door, unseen by the guests in the function rooms or workers who'd all be busy in the kitchens. If my hypothetical person knew the location of the fuse box, it would be pretty simple to flick the circuit breaker and kill the lights, then slip outside again with no one the wiser.

"Is the staff car park out there?" I nodded at the door.

"Yes, but don't worry, you can park in the guest car park since you'll be with the wedding."

I glanced around the ceiling, trying to be surreptitious.

Obviously I was unsuccessful, because Greta asked what I was looking for.

"Just wondering if you had cameras here. I figured the police must have a lot of footage to go through from the night of the Yule Ball."

"Oh. No, not really. We really only have cameras in the lifts and the guest corridors, for security. Oh, and in the main foyer. Nothing down here in the staff areas, and nothing in the ballroom or other function rooms." She sighed. "I don't know how they're ever going to find that necklace."

Excellent. If she wanted to talk about the case, I was more than happy to oblige her. "I suppose they searched all these lockers?"

"Oh, yes. They dusted the fuse box for fingerprints, too, but I don't think they got anything useful." She gestured at the corridor we'd just come down, and I saw the fuse box on the wall between here and the kitchen. It had a place to fit a padlock, but there wasn't one. "They think someone ran down from upstairs to kill the lights that night."

I frowned. "That's a long way from the ballroom. Maybe someone who wasn't even at the ball let themselves in from outside. Much less chance of them being seen that way." Although, it would help if this hypothetical person had some prior knowledge of the hotel—otherwise how would they know where to go?

She glanced at the staff entry, so close—and apparently, so very insecure. That was the trouble with these old hotels. They didn't have the security that newer ones did.

Greta sighed. "Yes, you're probably right."

"I don't suppose there's any chance you have camera surveillance of the dock or the car park, do you?"

"Not of the dock, no. We do have a camera on the car park, though. I assume the police took the footage. I hope it helps them."

"Me too."

Greta looked at her watch. "Is there anything else I can show you?"

"No, this has been very helpful, thanks. I should let you get back to your work."

"I'll walk you back to the foyer."

"Oh, that's all right. I can go out here. I just walk around to the side to get to the visitors' car park, right?"

"Yep, just follow the path past the staff car park."

"Thanks. See you later!"

"Bye!" She headed off at a brisk walk, her heels tapping on the floor as she went.

I left the building, blinking in the sudden brightness of the sunshine as I emerged from the shadows of the delivery dock. There were about twenty cars in the staff car park, with room for twice that many. Would the mystery person who'd turned off the lights at the Yule Ball have parked there?

But if they knew the location of the fuse box, they probably knew enough about the hotel to know that the car park was under surveillance. I looked around until I located the camera, high up on one of the light poles.

Surely they wouldn't be stupid enough to get themselves caught on camera while they facilitated a theft?

So maybe it *was* someone who'd already been in the building. Unless they'd managed to slink through the bushes to avoid the camera. I sighed, fed up with myself and all the *maybes*. I simply didn't have enough facts yet. *Everything* was a maybe.

I unlocked my shiny new car and got in. While I was still sitting there, trying to figure out what else I could do to eliminate a maybe or two, a man who looked a lot like Tim strode across the car park in front of me towards a very fancy sports car.

Curtis would probably know what it was on sight. It looked like that kind of car—the kind that men daydreamed about. I was too far away to see the insignia, but I could tell from its sleek lines that it was likely to cost a lot more than the one I was sitting in, even though mine was brand new.

I started my engine and sat there waiting as Tim got into the car and reversed neatly out of his spot. Was *that* the car he was driving around Australia in? I'd pictured something a lot more beat up, maybe even a van with a mattress in the back for sleeping rough. When people said they were on a working holiday, I assumed a backpacker level of luxury—doing things on the cheap, working as you went because you *had* to, because that was the only way you could afford the trip.

No backpacker ever drove a car that glided so smoothly on its state-of-the-art suspension, or whose engine had quite such a throaty, powerful growl. Curious to see what else I could find out about our mystery man, I pulled out of my spot and followed at a discreet distance.

Something wasn't adding up here, and Tim the bartender had just boosted himself to the top of my suspect list.

CHAPTER 11

I WAS RIGHT BEHIND HIM WHEN WE STOPPED AT SUNNY BAY'S one and only traffic light. His car was a Porsche, and even *I* knew that they were very expensive.

The car behind me honked. The lights had changed and I waved apologetically as I took off, letting Tim pull ahead.

He was doing the speed limit, or near enough, which seemed almost miraculous in a young man driving a powerful sports car. Was Tim the Unexpectedly Rich Bartender trying to avoid police notice? How very suspicious of him.

We came to a roundabout, and another car came in from the side and got in between us. That suited me just fine. The bright red Porsche was hard to miss. I wasn't going to lose him, unless perhaps he got on the freeway and headed to Newcastle or Sydney. But I didn't want him to notice the little red Mazda on his tail, so I was happy to sit back a bit.

Not that I'd follow him all the way to Newcastle or Sydney, if that was where he was going. But I suspected he was probably going home, and I was keen to see where Suspicious Tim called home. If it was as ritzy as his car I wouldn't know what to think.

Well, I'd think he made a habit of stealing expensive necklaces to fund his lifestyle, most likely. I'd think maybe there was a reason he kept moving from town to town, and it was nothing to do with sightseeing. But I was trying not to jump to conclusions. I needed facts first. Conclusions could come later.

When we got to Waterloo Bay, he turned off the main road that would eventually have taken him out to the freeway and headed into the main part of town. I slowed down, worried that I'd miss a turn, and saw him slide smoothly into a parking spot not far from the cinema.

I dumped my car in the first parking space I could find, anxious that I'd lose him, and jumped out.

A quick scan of the street failed to reveal any well-built young men with dark hair. Where was Rufus when I needed him? He could have tracked him down.

Oh, who was I kidding? Rufus would have wagged blankly at me, then wandered off in pursuit of his own interests. I loved that dog, but he was no bloodhound.

I hurried towards Tim's car. He couldn't have gone far, surely? Perhaps he was in the cinemas, buying a movie ticket. A quick peek into the foyer nixed that idea. I kept walking, but slowed down to give myself time to check out the interior of each shop as I passed. He must be in one of them—it was too far to the corner for him to have made it there without my seeing where he went.

I hit the jackpot at Carole's Café and Bakery. He was inside, approaching a woman sitting in a booth with her back to the street. She looked up when he stopped beside her and I saw it was Flick. Curiouser and curiouser. She hadn't seemed at all happy to see him when he'd bailed her up outside the ball. Why would she have agreed to a second meeting?

Because this had to be a meeting. He'd driven directly here, parked, gone inside, and gone straight to her. This was no chance encounter.

I followed him in, carefully not looking their way as I slid into a booth of my own. There was one between us, which was occupied by a couple of women chatting over coffee. Pretending to peruse the menu, I watched Tim and Flick over the top of it. They both looked tense. A waitress approached them and Tim smiled at her as he ordered. He really was handsome. I could see why Emily was interested.

Was it possible I had this all wrong, and he and Flick were actually a couple? Maybe Geraldine had looked so steamed at seeing them together because she didn't approve of her daughter carrying on a relationship with a lowly bartender. Mothers could certainly form strong opinions on the people their daughters were dating. Look at Priya's mum. She was obsessed with seeing her daughter happily settled with a suitable man.

I ignored the usual twinge of guilt that came whenever

I thought about Priya and the Great Boyfriend Scam. All I'd done was introduce them, the rest had been Priya's brainchild. Right now I had more important things to focus on.

The same waitress headed over to me next, and I ordered a latte, then pulled out my phone and pretended to be engrossed in my messages. The subterfuge was unnecessary, though. Flick and Tim seemed to have forgotten that anyone else existed. Tim certainly wasn't looking in my direction. Their conversation was low and intense.

I could catch the occasional word, but given the distance, and the other conversation going on at the booth between us, it was more tantalising than helpful. Geraldine's name came up, but I didn't hear what Flick said in reply.

They certainly weren't acting like two people in a relationship. There was no handholding across the table, no fond looks or flirty smiles. In fact, there were no smiles of any kind. Flick had her back to me, so I only got the occasional glimpse of her expression when she turned her head, but Tim's expression was serious and a little stressed.

Was he blackmailing her? Perhaps he'd stolen the necklace for her, and now he was threatening to reveal her part in the affair unless she gave him more money. I frowned down at my phone. How could he reveal her role without dobbing himself in at the same time? That didn't make sense.

The waitress brought my latte and I stirred sugar into

it thoughtfully. The ladies at the booth between us gathered up their things and left and I stared into the frothy milk on top of my coffee, straining to hear over the noise of their departure.

"... *my* ring," Flick said with a little heat as she sat back, with one arm resting on the back of the booth. She stared out the front window of the café, not looking at her companion.

Tim leaned closer and spoke quickly, looking very earnest. I didn't catch a word. What ring was she talking about? And why were they talking about rings at all? Maybe this wasn't the first time they'd pulled off a jewellery heist. Maybe they were a regular team and the necklace was just the most recent in a long line of thefts.

I frowned into my cup. That didn't make sense. Geraldine was loaded and Flick had always had the best of everything, according to Heidi. Why on earth would someone who already had more money than she could ever hope to spend be running around stealing jewellery? For kicks? Surely not. The reason she wanted *this* necklace in particular was because it was her dead father's gift to her mother. She wasn't just running around stealing necklaces willy-nilly.

As for Tim—his car made him look suspicious, but I supposed he might have come by his money honestly. Perhaps his parents had both died and left him a fortune. Or maybe he was a highly successful businessman.

Although, why would a successful businessman be taking a job as a bartender?

Had Tim just said he was hoping for more? I straightened up, conscious that I was leaning over my table at a ridiculous angle in my efforts to eavesdrop. I didn't want Tim noticing the crazy lady's focus on his meeting.

How much could he expect to get for a stolen necklace? If he'd stolen it for Flick, surely they'd discussed payment before now. Or maybe they had, and now he wasn't happy with the amount and was trying to get more out of her.

Did that mean that I'd found the thieves? The few crumbs of conversation I was picking up certainly sounded incriminating, but I was confused. If he'd handed over the necklace outside the ballroom, as I suspected, he no longer had any leverage to get more money out of his client. A clever thief would have held onto the goods if they planned on raising the price. If Flick wanted it badly enough, she would probably have paid whatever he was asking.

What could he do now to exert pressure on her? It wasn't as if he could go to the authorities—or even Geraldine—and tell them that Flick had the necklace. Anything he said would incriminate himself. And an anonymous tip accusing Geraldine's own daughter wouldn't hold any water with the police.

If only I could hear better! But the café was busy and the hum of conversation in the background was too loud. Tim was leaning forward, eyes fixed on Flick's face, clearly in the middle of an impassioned plea. I considered going to the bathroom so I'd have an excuse to wander past their table, but even that would only give me a snatch of their conversation—and it was far too likely they'd notice me and clam up anyway.

"I need more time!"

That was loud enough for me and half the café to catch. Flick slid out of her seat, casting a look of barely suppressed fury at Tim. She leaned closer and hissed, "I never asked for any of this. It's not fair."

Then she spun on her heel and stormed out. I watched her go, then rested my forehead on my hand and looked down so I wasn't staring directly at Tim. I'd caught a glimpse of his expression first, though, and he looked steamed.

A moment later he stood up, too, and stalked over to the cash register to pay. I watched his rigid back and wondered. What did Flick need more time for? What wasn't fair? Was she complaining about the police investigation?

If she was, she was a prize ninny, as Aunt Evie would have said. What did she expect to happen when her mother's necklace went missing? Did she think everyone would just say, *oh, well, it's gone, such a shame, carry on*? Of course there'd be an investigation, even if, as Curtis said, they didn't have much hope of actually finding the missing jewellery.

Why be angry about that? All she had to do was sit tight until it blew over and the necklace was hers forever. Admittedly, she'd have to be *super* careful about where she wore it in the future, but that was always going to be the case.

As I drained the last of my latte and prepared to head home, another thought occurred to me. *I never asked for this* was a very strange thing to say for someone who'd orchestrated the whole thing.

I sighed. I was never going to figure this out.

CHAPTER 12

ON THE WAY HOME, I DROPPED IN TO SEE AUNT EVIE. SHE always cheered me up when I was feeling despondent.

"This is a nice surprise!" she cried when she opened the door and found me on her doorstep. "Come in, come in. I'll put the kettle on."

Aunt Evie was a lot like Rufus in some ways. It didn't matter how recently she'd seen me, she always acted as if my arrival was the most marvellous thing that had happened to her in years. Her enthusiasm gave me a warm feeling inside.

"How did your Christmas shopping go yesterday?" she asked as she pottered around the kitchen. "Did you find something for Maisie?"

I told her about the book of fairy tales while the kettle bubbled merrily in the background and she measured tea leaves into her sturdy blue "everyday" teapot. She had a whole collection of teapots, some small, some large, including a silver one she kept for "best", which I'd never seen her use in my whole life. She said she was saving it in case royalty came to visit. Or George Clooney.

"I worry about that little girl," she said as we sat down at her scarred old kitchen table by the window.

"About Maisie? Why?"

"That awful mother of hers. Curtis is marvellous, of course. You couldn't ask for a more devoted dad. But Kelly." She shook her head. "Well, you know what it's like to grow up without a mother. A little girl needs her mum. And Kelly might as well be dead for all the attention she pays to that little sweetheart. It's such a shame. I'm sure I don't know how Maisie turned out as sweet as she is with a mother like that." She smiled at me. "Must be Curtis's genes."

It was true that Curtis had won the genetic lottery. Maisie would probably grow up to be a real stunner, with two such good-looking parents.

"I've only met Kelly once. I can't say I was impressed."

"No, she wouldn't have seen any point in being nice to you. She can charm birds out of the trees if she sees some advantage to herself in it. Half the men in this town are infatuated with her. They should know better, but men often aren't thinking with their brains where a pretty woman is concerned, are they?"

"Aunt *Evie*!"

She grinned and passed me the plate of biscuits. I took one with an orange cream filling.

"Anyway, I'm glad you've got something nice for Maisie. It will be good for her, having a woman around to make a fuss of her."

"I'm sure her grandmothers dote on her."

"Oh, yes, them." Aunt Evie waved a hand, dismissing all grandmothers from consideration. "That's not the same thing, though, is it? Silly Kelly, so focused on making money. I wonder if she'll look back one day and regret not valuing her daughter more highly?"

I didn't think Kelly was the type for regrets, but I shrugged. "Rich people are a different breed."

"And speaking of rich people," she said, "how is your investigation going?"

"Why? Has Geraldine been asking?"

"Goodness, no. Geraldine and I don't chat beyond arranging the auction. We don't move in the same circles at all. I was just hoping you might have some news for me."

"No." There was no point going into my suspicions. I was still desperately short on actual evidence, and I didn't want to get Aunt Evie's hopes up for nothing. "But since you brought it up, do you know where Geraldine lives?"

"Yes, of course. Not far from here, actually. She's got a big house up on Pacific Parade. Why?"

"I thought I'd go to see her. Ask some questions, you know."

Aunt Evie raised one eyebrow. "No, I don't know. What do you want to ask Geraldine questions about? Her safe?"

"Just a couple of things to do with the investigation."

"You're being very mysterious! What kind of things? Do you think Flick did it?"

I smiled to soften my refusal. "Nothing exciting. I just want to clear up a few details." Like why she had a face like a thunder cloud when she saw her daughter talking to Tim the bartender.

"You must be making *some* progress with your investigation, then?"

Aunt Evie was normally very good at wheedling information out of me, but this time I held firm. I really didn't think we had a chance of seeing that necklace again.

Aunt Evie got up and disappeared into her bedroom for a moment. When she came back she was carrying her address book, a well-thumbed floral notebook that had been with her as long as I could remember. Aunt Evie was one of the few people I knew who still had such a thing. Like me, everyone else kept contact details in their phones.

She had brought a small memo pad with her, too. She sat down and flipped to the Ws. "Here it is. 72 Pacific Parade. I'll just write it down for you so you don't forget."

"Thanks."

Aunt Evie had the most beautiful handwriting—probably from all those years of having to write things down, like addresses in address books. Her letters were round and perfectly formed, and flowed together in a continuous chain of elegant loops. I folded the piece of paper in half and tucked it into my back pocket.

"It's no trouble. I had to look up the address myself anyway. I'm going to send her some flowers as a thank-you on behalf of the organising committee."

"Oh, don't worry," I said, seeing an opportunity. "I can pick up some flowers from Denise's for you tomorrow and deliver them in person."

Aunt Evie's eyes sparkled. "Good idea. Then she won't be suspicious when you start asking questions." She gave me a fond smile. "You're a natural at this investigation stuff. And to think, you were the most guileless child. I always knew when you were lying because you blushed."

"You make me sound like some master of deception," I protested. "All I'm going to do is ask the woman a couple of questions. It's not as though I'm trying to pull off some grand heist."

No, where grand heists were concerned, I suspected that Geraldine's daughter knew far more about such things than I did.

The next morning, Rufus and I were on Denise's doorstep at nine o'clock sharp. It was another beautiful sunny day in Sunrise Bay, with not a cloud in the sky, and it was already hot. Rufus's long pink tongue lolled out of his mouth as he panted.

"Sit," I told him at the door of Denise's shop.

For once, he was only too happy to oblige, flopping down onto the cool concrete outside her door like a dog that had just run a marathon, when all we had done was walk the ten minutes from home to the florist. Though, to be fair, Rufus had probably covered twice as much distance as I had as he ranged backward and forward, sniffing out all the good smells.

The bell over the door tinkled as I pushed it open and a wave of perfumed and blessedly air-conditioned air greeted me. I took a deep breath. I loved the smell of Denise's shop. It was like a breath of spring every time you walked in.

As it turned out, I wasn't her first customer of the day. To my surprise, none other than Tim the bartender was there before me, engaged in a long and apparently very serious conversation about the relative merits of tulips versus roses with Denise. She waved hello when she saw me but kept chatting. Tim didn't turn around.

I wandered around the shop while I waited, bending occasionally to sniff at a bucket of flowers. Denise had some gorgeous pink roses in, pale and perfect, but they didn't have much of a scent. In contrast, the red ones next to them smelled like an English country garden, ripe with the promise of summer.

"Where are we sending these?" Denise asked with her pen poised over her paperwork.

"72 Pacific Parade," Tim said.

My ears pricked up at that. Who was he sending flowers to? Geraldine or Flick? Neither of them seemed particularly likely. How funny that we were both here to buy flowers for the same address. Both of us had an agenda, too, I was willing to bet.

Tim was wearing a pair of jeans and an open-necked shirt that was tailored to fit him like a glove. A lot of people in Sunny Bay wore sandals or no shoes at all at this time of year, but I couldn't help noticing that Tim had on a pair of very stylish loafers. In fact his whole look was more *man about town* than *broke tourist*. He dressed like a man who drove a Porsche, in fact. I couldn't help feeling that there was something mighty fishy about our handsome bartender.

"Name?" Denise asked.

"Tim Li."

"You're sending flowers to a Mr Tim Li?"

"Oh, sorry." He gave an awkward chuckle. "I thought you meant *my* name. No, the flowers are for Felicity Winderbaum."

"How lovely! I'm sure she'll be thrilled."

I grinned to myself. I bet she wouldn't be. She and Tim had hardly parted on good terms yesterday.

"Is it a special occasion?" Denise asked.

"No."

Ha. A man of few words. Funny, he'd seemed to have plenty to say yesterday in the café. Much good it had done him. I hung back, hoping that Denise would be able to draw him out.

"Would you like a complementary card? To write a message in," she added when he gave her a blank look.

He nodded. "Yes, please."

Denise indicated the selection of cards by the cash register. "Pick any of those." She handed him a pen and then got to work assembling the flowers they had agreed on. Apparently the luscious pink roses had won the day.

"How are you, Charlie?" she asked, her hands busy with her task.

I moved up to the counter, using it as an excuse to get closer to Tim. "I'm good, thanks."

Tim had selected a card and was now frowning at the blank white interior of it. The words didn't seem to be coming. I wondered what his endgame was here. He could hardly write, *Sorry for trying to extort you, let's still be friends.* What was the point of the flowers? Maybe I had it all wrong and they *were* lovers, despite appearances to the contrary at the café. I supposed even the happiest couples did fight occasionally.

"Hey, you're the bartender," I said cheerily. "I met you at the ball on Wednesday night, remember?"

"Oh, right," he said with a distinct lack of enthusiasm. "Hello again."

"He's driving around Australia," I told Denise. "Isn't that right?"

"Yeah."

"Where did you start from?" Denise asked, her smile bright as she wrangled roses and baby's breath and stems of bright green foliage. I looked away. I'd seen enough of Denise's rose arrangements to last me a lifetime when my persistent ex-fiancé had been trying to win me back with incessant deliveries.

"Sydney." Tim fiddled with the pen.

"Really?" Denise laughed. "You haven't got far, then."

He smiled, but it seemed like a bit of an effort. "Sunrise Bay seemed like such a nice place, I thought I'd stop for a while. There's no rush."

Denise nodded enthusiastically. "You're right about that. It *is* a lovely place, isn't it, Charlie? Charlie's pretty new in town, too."

"Yeah?"

"I moved up here from Sydney a couple of months ago," I said. "Do you surf?"

I needed to get the conversation back to Tim. If I didn't jump in, Denise would tell him the whole history of my move here and the saga with Will trying to convince me to take him back, for which she had had a ringside seat.

Tim looked at me blankly. "Surf?"

Was that a difficult question? Sunny Bay was a beach-side town—there wasn't a lot else to do here besides go to the beach.

"A lot of people come here for the waves," I said. "Apparently it's a good surf beach. I just thought that must have been why you decided to stop here."

I hoped he might take the conversational bait and run with it, but he stonewalled me.

"No, I'm not a surfer. I don't like swimming."

"Then what made you decide to stay?" I asked. Might as well come straight out and ask him.

He shrugged. "The people seem nice."

What a dodgy answer. Which people? Geraldine? Because she sure hadn't been nice to him. Neither had her daughter. If he was actually in a relationship with Flick, it was time to head for the lifeboats.

He half-turned his back to me and held his pen poised to write, making it clear he wasn't interested in further conversation. I folded my arms and checked on Rufus, who was still obediently sitting outside. What a good boy. I'd have to give him an extra treat when we got home.

I noticed Tim's car on the other side of the street. A couple of guys had stopped to admire its sleek lines.

"Is that your car over the road?" I asked.

Reluctantly, he cast a glance over his shoulder. "Yep."

"Pretty fancy for driving around Australia. I hope

you're not planning to take any unsealed roads in that thing."

He grunted, focused on the card. He was writing something, but no matter how I craned my neck I couldn't read the message. He had his writing covered by his left hand, like a school kid trying to protect their test from being copied.

The watch on his left wrist looked like something James Bond might have worn. It had a gleaming gold band and a lot of expensive-looking dials on its face. Pricey car. Pricey watch. This guy either had a lot of money, or he was a professional thief. He was supposedly on a road trip to see the country, but he'd chosen to stop long enough in a coastal town to get himself a job. And he didn't even like swimming.

There was something very fishy about Mr Tim Li.

CHAPTER 13

HALF AN HOUR LATER, I WAS PARKING MY CAR OUTSIDE THE enormous mansion at 72 Pacific Parade. Rufus had given me a betrayed look when I'd grabbed the car keys and started to leave without him, but all had been forgiven when I'd given him a bone to munch on while I was gone. Geraldine didn't look like the kind of person who would appreciate a visit from an ambulant lump of shedding fur.

Her house looked like it should have been perched on a mountain somewhere in Canada, serving as a lodge for wealthy tourists in some alpine paradise. Maybe even a small hotel. The house was twice as big as any other house in the street, and they were all huge. The entire façade was covered in beautiful grey stone, and the windows in the central part of the house where the front doors were stretched two storeys high.

I mounted the stone steps to the imposing double doors, which were as oversized as the windows, and knocked, juggling the bunch of flowers I'd bought in my other arm. I'd chosen the tulips, since I was a little over roses—and besides, Flick would be getting a delivery of roses soon. It would be nice for Geraldine to get something different.

Geraldine opened the door, smiling when she saw the flowers.

"Oh, are those for me?"

"Yes. They're from the Yule Ball committee, to say thank you again for your generosity."

She accepted them happily. "How lovely. Tulips are my favourite flowers. How clever of Evelyn to find that out."

I didn't volunteer that Aunt Evie had had nothing to do with the choice of flowers, and it was pure chance that they were her favourites. It might make her more inclined to be helpful if she thought that Aunt Evie was devoting her time to pleasing Geraldine.

"You're her niece, aren't you? You were at the ball."

"That's right." I opened my bag and pulled out the photo that I'd brought. "I thought you might like a copy of this photo."

It was the one I'd taken of her shaking hands with Stellan just before the lights went out. The sapphire necklace was still safely on its stand in the background.

Her smile faded as she examined the photo. "Such a shame about that necklace. It was such a beautiful piece."

"The police could still find it," I said bracingly.

"I can't believe it could disappear so quickly," she said, her gaze pensive.

"Do you have any thoughts on that?" I asked.

She looked up, frowning. "What do you mean?"

"Any idea who could have taken it, or how?"

"I'm sure I don't know." She turned her frown back on the photo. "Although I did wonder ..."

"What?" I prompted when she trailed off.

She gestured at Stellan in the photo. "After all, *he* was the closest, wasn't he? Who else could have reached it in time without being caught?"

I refrained from pointing out that Geraldine herself was just as close, since I didn't really think she'd stolen her own necklace.

"The police did search him," I said instead. "Pretty thoroughly, too."

"Oh, well, I suppose they couldn't be all that thorough, in the circumstances." She gave a little fake laugh. "They couldn't exactly strip-search people, could they?"

Judging by the smirk on her face, I suspected she was imagining Curtis conducting a strip search.

I frowned. "I think they're looking at another suspect —a guy who works at the hotel. I believe you know him. His name's Tim." Two bright spots of colour appeared on her cheeks at his name, as if even thinking of him made her mad. "How do you know him?"

"I really don't."

"Why don't you like him?"

Her eyes sparked with anger and for a moment I thought she would slam the door in my face. "That's none of your business."

"But it could have a bearing on the theft."

"He's just a nasty little gold digger," she burst out, "trying to get my daughter's money."

I blinked. "They're in a relationship?" It certainly hadn't looked that way.

Geraldine looked revolted. "Certainly not!"

A car pulled into the driveway, rather faster than seemed safe. Flick got out and slammed the door.

"Well, thank you for delivering these," Geraldine said, obviously meaning for me to leave.

I took a step away from the door, watching Flick take the stairs two at a time. Her lovely face was twisted into a scowl, and she didn't seem to notice me standing there. I took another step back. Something told me this wasn't a good time to get between Flick and her goal, which was clearly her mother.

"Darling, what's wrong?" Geraldine asked.

"You *lied* to me," Flick snarled.

Geraldine's expression changed, going from concern to outrage in the blink of an eye.

"You've been with that man, haven't you?" Her frown matched her daughter's now, and the family resemblance was far more obvious than usual. "I warned you. I *told* you not to have anything to do with him. He's only after money."

Oh, this was good. I shrank back against the wall, hoping that they'd both forget I was there. Were they talking about Tim?

"He's got more money than you, Mum! He's got more money than *God*." She was almost shouting now, and if looks could kill, Geraldine would have been writhing on the doormat in her death throes. "He doesn't need your money. That's not what it's about, but that's all you ever think about, isn't it? As if he would want money from us when he's got all my father's money. You made a big mistake when you let Dad go, didn't you? You should have tried for more in the divorce settlement."

Geraldine's mouth had thinned into an angry line. "You have no business saying such things."

"Well, you had no business keeping secrets from me my whole life, either, but here we are. Why didn't you tell me I had a half-brother?"

Geraldine tried for a soothing tone, though I could tell it was an effort. "We should discuss this later."

"What's to discuss?" Flick demanded. "I am never speaking to you again."

She shoved past her mother and stormed into the house. Her heels tap-tap-tapped across the foyer, the only sound in the sudden awkward silence.

"I should go," I said, though I was burning up with questions.

Geraldine was still holding the flowers. The cellophane wrapping crackled and I realised she was practically crushing them.

"Sometimes I wonder why I bothered having children. So *ungrateful*. You should think about that, Marley, before you decide to devote *years* of your life to raising them."

She sounded so bitter I didn't even correct her.

"That young man. Tim Li." She said his name as though it tasted bad. "You might have seen him at the Yule Ball. This is all *his* fault."

"I did. He was working the bar."

"Yes." She met my eyes briefly, and hers were smouldering. "He's the son of my second husband, Max. Oh, *why* couldn't he just *stay away*?"

"His arrival seems to have caused quite a stir."

"Stupid, selfish boy. He's as bad as his mother."

"Who's his mother?" It was the most diplomatic thing I could think of, because I was getting the strong impression that Tim might have been the reason that Max Li became Geraldine's *ex*-husband.

"Max's second wife."

"Oh." So much for my strong impression. Unless …

"I know what you're thinking." She sighed and her shoulders slumped. The cellophane crackled again as she loosened her grip. "But it wasn't like that. Max and I were very different people, and we simply fell out of love. We got divorced, and the following year he met Eileen. They got married and Tim arrived a year later. He's three years younger than Flick."

I frowned. "But she didn't know he existed?"

That seemed odd. If the divorce had been amicable, wouldn't Max have stayed in Flick's life? So how had the arrival of a half-sibling been kept a secret?

"Unfortunately, Max and Eileen didn't stay married for long. Less than a year after Tim was born, they split, and this time it wasn't friendly. Eileen was very bitter and wouldn't let Max see the baby."

"Surely he could have challenged her in court?"

"Perhaps he would have, if he'd lived."

I blinked. "He died?"

"Yes. He went out for a run one day and never returned. No one realised, but he had a heart condition. He

SANTA, SURF AND SAPPHIRES

was one of those people who looked so fit on the outside, you could never imagine that there was something wrong on the inside. It took the police a few days to figure out who he was, because he had no ID on him when his body was found. Eventually someone reported him missing and then they put the pieces together."

"That must have been a terrible shock."

She nodded gravely. "It was a great shock to us all. Max was the last person you would pick to simply fall down dead one day."

"That doesn't explain why you didn't tell Flick about Tim, though."

"I went to the reading of his will." Her eyes had a distant look. Remembering. "When the solicitor called me to tell me I was a beneficiary, I assumed Max had set up some sort of trust for Flick. She was his only daughter, after all, and one of his two children. But he'd left me some knickknack."

"What about Flick?"

She shook her head. "Nothing. Can you believe that? He was one of the richest men in the country, and I hadn't remarried yet. Money was tight, and all he left me was a stupid little statue that he knew I didn't like. Nothing for Flick at all, as if she didn't even exist."

"So who got all his money? Tim?"

"No. He'd left everything to Eileen. Every last cent."

Flick had said Tim had all his father's money. Did that mean Eileen was dead now, too?

"I went to see her, to demand justice for my daughter," she continued. "But Eileen refused to give me a single cent. She actually laughed in my face. Can you believe that?" Her breast swelled in indignation at the memory. "So I cut her and her stupid son out of our lives. She wanted to pretend Flick didn't exist? Fine. Two could play at that game."

"Why would he leave all his money to Eileen if they weren't even speaking?"

Geraldine shrugged. "He probably hadn't gotten around to changing his will. Anyway, apparently Eileen didn't tell Tim about Flick, either. Didn't think it was important, probably. She never liked me, and always acted as if Max's first marriage had never happened. But she passed away recently, and his stepfather told him he had a half-sister, and the first thing he did was drive up here and try to see Flick."

"Wow." What a stressful time for the poor guy. To lose your mum and then discover the existence of a sibling you'd never met. That was intense. I'd be pretty keen to meet them, too.

"He came to the house, but I sent him away with a flea in his ear. As if a few smiles could make up for his mother leaving us *destitute*."

I had a feeling that Geraldine's idea of *destitute* was a lot different to mine. If I were a betting kind of person, I'd put money on the fact that Geraldine had actually tried to keep Tim away for a totally different reason. She'd been afraid that Flick would react exactly as she just had to the news that her mother had kept such a secret from her.

Geraldine sighed. "But he was determined to meet her. When he showed up again at the Yule Ball, I tried to keep them apart, but I couldn't watch her every minute. He showed her Max's signet ring, to prove he was who he said he was. In fact, he gave it to her. She hadn't believed him at first, but she'd seen photos of that ring all her life. She was very upset, just as I knew she would be."

I nodded, but I was only half-listening. My mind had disappeared down a different track. The ring must have been what I saw Tim pass to Flick outside the ballroom. That was why she'd looked so shocked. A perfect stranger had just told her he was her half-brother.

It was nothing to do with the stolen sapphire necklace at all. And Tim driving an expensive car no longer seemed suspicious. If he had all his father's money, of course he had a fancy car and ritzy-looking watch. He wasn't on a trip around Australia at all. Everything he'd done made sense in light of this new information.

And my whole case had just gone up in smoke.

CHAPTER 14

LATE SATURDAY AFTERNOON, MY DOORBELL RANG. CURTIS wasn't due for another two hours, and I wasn't expecting anyone. Thinking it might be Aunt Evie, I was surprised to find Jack on the doorstep instead.

"Hi," I said. "What's up? You look stressed."

Jack was quite possibly the most laidback person I'd ever met. I mean, how much more laidback could you be than to casually agree to pretend to be someone's boyfriend as if it were no big deal to face down a whole family? I'd often seen him exhausted. Shift work did that to a person. But I'd never seen him without his sunny smile.

Right now, that smile had gone walkabout.

"Could you do me a favour?" he asked.

"Sure. What do you need?"

He grabbed my hand and tugged me out the door. Rufus came, too, wagging happily. Jack was one of his favourite people, but Jack didn't even acknowledge him, much less shower him with his usual affection. That was how I knew this was serious.

"I can't decide what to wear." He dragged me through the garden and into his house, which was the mirror reverse of mine.

"What to wear?" I followed him up the stairs to the bedroom level, Rufus padding along behind us.

"To my date with Priya tonight."

I laughed. Had his conscience finally caught up with him? "Surely the master deceiver isn't nervous about spending the evening *lying* to Priya's whole family?"

"Don't be like that," he said. "I can't afford to stuff this up. Priya will never forgive me."

His bed was strewn with shirts in different colours and several different pairs of trousers. It looked like he'd emptied out his whole wardrobe.

Settled comfortably on one pillow was Sherlock, apparently overseeing the entire operation. He blinked slowly at me, then froze as Rufus followed me into the room. Rufus didn't even notice the black cat for a moment, but when he did he came right up to the bed, wagging cautiously, and sniffed at him. Sherlock looked affronted.

"Aww, look at that," Jack said. "They're buddies."

Sherlock was watching Rufus, his green eyes narrowed in suspicion. I wouldn't have said they were buddies, but at least Sherlock was tolerating having a dog in his domain. Said dog, of course, was completely oblivious to the fact that small, black cats might not be as enthusiastic about being friends with large, boisterous dogs as those dogs might wish. But after another sniff, he left Sherlock alone and sprawled out on the bedroom floor just where he was guaranteed to be most in Jack's way.

Jack ran a hand through his curly dark hair, which was standing up at even wilder angles than usual, as if he'd been doing that for a while. "I keep trying things on, but nothing looks quite right."

I folded my arms. "Nothing looks right for swindling a bunch of innocent people, you mean?"

"Charlie, please! I'm desperate here. Throw a guy a bone."

"Fine." I picked up a light green shirt with small pink flowers on it. "What about this one?"

"Too informal."

I put that one back and selected a plain shirt in a deep blue. "It's only family dinner, not a black-tie event. How about this one, then? It's less beachy."

I held it up against him. It looked fine. More than fine, really. He was an attractive guy, though not the type to turn heads on the street. But his eyes were a beautiful green—rather like his cat's, actually—his beard was neatly trimmed, and when he was smiling, as he usually was, his expression was open and friendly.

But right now he was frowning. "I don't know. Dark blue reminds me too much of work."

His nurses' scrubs were a mid-blue, but I knew the more senior staff wore navy. I sighed and hung the dark blue shirt back in the wardrobe. Rufus got up and sniffed at a pink shirt hanging half off the bed, wagging doubtfully.

"What about that one? Rufus seems to like it."

"I'm not sure I trust Rufus's fashion advice."

"Let me see it on you."

He dragged his T-shirt off before I even had time to turn away. He had nice shoulders. Probably lumping patients around all day built up muscles. He certainly wasn't shy about his body. Living in Sunny Bay tended to make people casual like that—any day of the week you could see vast expanses of flesh on display on the beach.

"What do you think?" he asked when he had the buttons done up. He turned to assess himself in the mirrored wardrobe door. "Does it make me look too pale?"

"I think it looks great. And Rufus is wagging, so obviously he agrees."

Finally a smile peeked out and Jack bent down to pat Rufus on the head. The wagging increased exponentially. "Good boy, Rufus."

"See? He's an expert fashion advisor."

Still Jack frowned at his reflection. "Do you think Priya will like it?"

I folded my arms again and gave him a stern look. At least, I tried to make it stern. Inside, a secret delight was bubbling. "Jack Watson. You're not worried about what Priya's family thinks at all, are you? All this fuss is about impressing *Priya*."

He looked down and fiddled with the top button of his shirt while a slow wave of colour crept up from under his beard. "I just don't want to let her down."

I shook my head. "You know you could have just asked her to go out with you. You didn't have to agree to this ridiculous scheme of hers."

"We'd just met! She didn't know the first thing about me. I'd look like a weirdo if I asked her out. And then she asked me to do this and I couldn't just leave her hanging," he said. "Why would she go out with me after I'd refused to help her?"

"I don't know, because she admired your principles and moral fortitude?"

He gave me a level stare. "Turning a girl down is *not* the way to impress her."

"So you admit you want to impress her?"

"What is this, the Spanish Inquisition?"

I laughed. "*Nobody* expects the Spanish Inquisition."

"Exactly."

His front door bell pealed and he gave me a stricken look. "Oh, no, is that her already?"

"She's picking you up?"

"Yeah, at five-thirty. Her dad likes an early dinner."

My watch said it was only five-fifteen. "She's a little early. Want me to get that while you finish getting ready?"

"Thanks."

Rufus and I headed downstairs and opened the door. It was indeed Priya, looking gorgeous in a hot pink silk shirt and black pants.

"Hello," she said. "What are you doing here?"

"Dealing with a wardrobe crisis. Jack couldn't decide what to wear."

Her eyebrows shot up as she stepped inside. "And did you manage to save the day?"

"Well, it was Rufus, really." I patted his fluffy head. "He has quite the eye."

She laughed, clearly not believing me.

"You may laugh, but wait until you see what he picked out. You guys are going to match."

"Be there in a sec!" Jack called, and a moment later he appeared at the top of the stairs. He had the sleeves of his Rufus-approved pink shirt rolled to the elbow, exposing his tanned forearms, and his top button was undone. The shirt hung loose over dark blue chinos. He hurried down the stairs, bringing a wave of aftershave with him. "You look fabulous," he said to Priya as he leaned in and kissed the air beside her cheek. "Am I too casual?"

"No, you look great," she assured him. To me, she added, "I see what you mean."

I grinned. "Your mother is going to think you guys colour coordinated your outfits."

"I'll tell her we didn't and it's just this great chemistry we have," she said.

I shook my head. "You are shameless."

She shrugged. "*Shameless* is my middle name."

"Gotta find my keys," Jack said. "Back in a minute."

He disappeared into the kitchen and Priya made herself at home on his big leather couch.

"How's your investigation going?" she asked.

I groaned. "Terrible. I lost my main suspects yesterday. I don't know how I'm going to tell Aunt Evie."

"Lost them? What do you mean?"

I told her all about Tim and Flick and their long-dead daddy's ring while she made noises of shock and commiseration in all the right places. Jack came back in during the telling and listened with just as much interest.

"So all their suspicious meetings and stuff had nothing to do with the necklace?" he asked.

"Yeah."

"Flick still might have done it, though. If she wanted that necklace badly enough. He might even have helped, if he was trying to get on her good side."

I gave him a flat stare. "Yeah, guys do stupid things sometimes when they're trying to impress a woman."

He coloured a little and cleared his throat. "Well, don't give up, anyway. You'll figure it out."

"Yeah," Priya said. "There must be other suspects. Who else was close enough to grab the necklace in the dark?"

"Well, the auctioneer."

She laughed. "Jeff Borello? He's been mayor forever. He's squeaky clean."

"Unless he's being pressured into a life of crime because he owes money to someone dangerous," Jack suggested.

We both stared at him.

"What?" He sounded defensive. "It could happen."

"Sometimes there's corruption on local councils," I said. "Just because he's mayor doesn't make him a saint."

Priya snorted. "Jeff wouldn't even owe money in library fines. He's *that* kind of a guy. Who else?"

"Geraldine was the next closest," I said, giving up on the mayor idea. Priya would know.

That earned another snort. "You've got to be kidding. You think she'd steal back her own necklace?"

"No. I'm just saying, she was close."

Priya waved her hand in airy dismissal of Geraldine. "I only want to hear about people who were close who might possibly be our *suspect*. What about Stellan? He was standing right next to Geraldine."

"He seems pretty unlikely, too," Jack objected. "He'd just won the auction."

"So?" Priya shrugged. "Maybe he had buyer's remorse."

"Geraldine's son Phil did drive the price up," I said.

"See?" She cast a triumphant glance at Jack, as if he'd been arguing with her. "He didn't want to pay an inflated price for it, but he still wanted it, so he decided to just take it. That's way more likely than Geraldine deciding to pocket it."

"Except he was searched," Jack said.

"So was everyone," I pointed out, "but someone still took it."

"Okay, say it's Stellan," he said. "How did he get it out without the police finding it? They're not stupid. They know as well as we do that he had one of the best opportunities. They were pretty thorough."

"You know," Priya said, "when Rakesh was a little boy, Mum took us into a big toy shop in Newcastle. She was shopping for a birthday present for one of my cousins."

I frowned in confusion. "Okaaay. Why is it suddenly story time?"

"Bear with me," she said. "I'm getting there. So they had all these little cars on display inside a glass counter. Rakesh was so small he could barely see over the top of it. He stood there with his nose practically pressed up against the glass, and he started whining and begging for one of them for himself. Mum ignored him, of course. She was never the type to buy us random treats."

"I think I see where this is going," Jack said with a grin.

She smiled back at him. "So the sales guy had all these cars out on the counter, showing Mum, including the little red one that Rakesh really wanted. She took her time choosing, and a couple of other kids came up to the counter next to us to have a look, too. The sales guy was keeping a close eye on them.

"Anyway, Mum chose the ones she wanted, and the sales guy started putting the others away, and suddenly he stops, and says, where's the red one gone? He and Mum looked all around the counter and even on the floor, but eventually he decided that one of the kids who'd been next to us must have taken it while he wasn't looking. He said that kind of thing happened all the time and he was really cranky about it."

"Are you saying *Rakesh* took it?" I could hardly believe it. I'd met Priya's little brother, and he was a stand-up guy.

Her smile broke into a laugh. "His one and only foray into crime. He realised once he got it home that he could never play with it in case Mum noticed."

"Proving that crime doesn't pay," Jack said.

"But how did he manage to get it home without your mum seeing it?" I asked.

"Shoved it up the leg of his shorts and tucked it into his undies."

Jack laughed. "And there's another reason he could never play with it."

Priya's dark eyes gleamed with amusement. "Not the most hygienic solution, I admit, but it worked. Anyway, my point is that Stellan could have done something similar."

"Shoved a sapphire necklace into his undies?" I hovered between laughter and horror. "I watched Curtis pat him down in front of the whole ballroom. Surely he would have noticed?"

"Not to get too graphic," Priya said with obvious enjoyment, "but Curtis didn't probe into *every* possible area a necklace could have been concealed."

"Yeah," Jack said. "A pat-down is a different thing to a full-on grope."

They grinned at each other and I shook my head. "You guys are gross. What a beautiful couple you make. Come on, Rufus, let's go home and leave these two to their big date."

I headed for the door.

Jack quirked an eyebrow at Priya. "Shall we?"

"Let's go!"

"Good luck." I waved goodbye as they headed to Priya's car. "Hope it's not a *complete* disaster."

"It'll be fine." Priya threw me a cheeky grin. "What could possibly go wrong?"

I shuddered. "Don't *say* that!"

CHAPTER 15

I OPENED MY DOOR AGAIN JUST BEFORE SEVEN, FEELING SUDDENLY breathless. "Hi!"

Curtis smiled at me, brown eyes warm, the crow's feet at the corners of them crinkling delightfully. "Hi. You look lovely."

"Thanks." I was wearing a new dress that I'd bought in Waterloo Bay, a pale blue halterneck that left my back bare, clung to my hips, then flared out into a full skirt that swished when I moved.

He looked pretty darn good himself as he leaned in to kiss me. He wore a white shirt that showed off his tan and dark blue jeans held up by a wide leather belt that had an ornate buckle. He looked like a cowboy—a really upmarket one—and he smelled divine, like sunshine and pine trees and fresh, open spaces.

Rufus decided that that was *quite* enough kissing, and surged out to say his own hellos, his tail bashing against my legs as he went. We broke apart, apologies on my lips and a smile on Curtis's.

"It's fine." He bent down to pat the dog, who gazed at him adoringly. I could understand that. I could stare at Curtis all day long, and often felt the urge to pinch myself to prove that I wasn't dreaming when that delectable dimple of his peeped out. "Are you ready to go?"

"Sure am." I shooed Rufus back inside, grabbed my bag, and shut the door in his aggrieved furry face. He didn't understand why he couldn't come with me as he usually did. But while the surf club café might not have minded having him lurking under their outdoor tables, I knew that the smart new restaurant we were visiting tonight wouldn't be as laidback.

Curtis walked close by me as we went down the driveway, one hand warm on my bare back. I wasn't a short woman, but I felt like a midget next to him. He was built on generous lines, not simply tall but muscled with it. When he was wearing his uniform, he cut an imposing figure. I bet any criminal faced with that much sheer physical power had second thoughts about their chosen profession.

He opened the passenger door of his four-wheel-drive, then shut it behind me. I was an independent woman, but I felt a secret thrill at being looked after like this. I couldn't help recalling Aunt Evie saying once, when I first moved to Sunrise Bay, *you deserve someone who will treasure you.* Was this what being treasured felt like? If so, I could get used to it.

"Where's Maisie tonight?" I asked as we headed down Beach Road. "With Kelly?"

"Yes." It was a big car, but the steering wheel still looked small under his large, capable hands. "Kelly's heading overseas on Monday, so she's got Maisie all this weekend instead."

I frowned. "But she'll be back for Christmas?" Christmas Day was a week away, and I couldn't imagine any mother wanting to spend it apart from her little girl—especially not when that little girl was as sweet as Maisie.

"Nope. She's spending Christmas skiing in Aspen with her new boyfriend." Whatever Curtis thought about that, his face gave nothing away.

"So you get Maisie to yourself?" I still couldn't quite get my head around it. If I was Kelly, I would have taken Maisie with me, but it worked in Curtis's favour this way. No arguments about who was going to spend Christmas Day with Maisie.

"Yes. Mum's coming over in the morning to watch her open her presents, and I'm planning a seafood lunch. Are you ... would you like to come? It's nothing fancy, just a chill kind of day. We might go to the beach afterwards."

"I'd love to." I was having dinner with Aunt Evie, but I'd made no plans for Christmas Day beyond sleeping in and watching corny Christmas movies on TV. "I'll bring dessert. Aunt Evie gave me the recipe for her famous pavlova."

His lips quirked. "The one that caused all the fuss at Sunrise Lodge a couple of months back?"

"That's the one."

"It certainly looked good. Although perhaps it should be called her *infamous* pavlova."

I laughed and we chatted comfortably all the way to Waterloo Bay. He took my hand as we walked from the car to the restaurant, lacing his fingers in between mine, and I sighed with contentment. Life was good.

The restaurant had carved wooden panels on the walls and lots of greenery—plants in sturdy pots in the corners, and trailing from hanging baskets. A burst of familiar laughter greeted me as we entered. Good heavens. I'd assumed that Priya's family dinner was being held at Amina's home, but no, there they all were, at a table in the centre of the small room: Amina and her husband Raul, their son Rakesh, and Priya and Jack. Jack had his arm loosely slung across the back of Priya's chair as she told some story that had the others all laughing, watching her with an indulgent smile. She caught sight of me as the waiter led us to a table for two in the corner and waved. I waved back and chose the seat that gave me a view of their table.

Amina leaned forward as I did so and patted Jack comfortably on the arm, as if they were old friends.

"Priya's scheme seems to have worked out," Curtis said, following my gaze as he took his own seat.

"Yes." But I couldn't feel relieved. Watching them all laughing and chatting together, I couldn't help feeling a sense of impending doom. Amina looked charmed by Jack, as well she might. He was a charming guy. I'd known him less than a month, but I was already very fond of him. Even Priya's dad, who'd spent most of the Yule Ball

looking vaguely bored, seemed animated, smiling and
nodding as he joined in the general chat. How would they
both feel if they found out this was all a scam?

"You look anxious," Curtis said. "Worried the truth
will come out?"

I smiled. "Exactly. I guess I don't need to tell you that
crime rarely pays."

He laughed as he took the menu the waiter was offering. "Thanks. I don't know that I'd call it *crime*, exactly."

"No. I suppose not." I stared at my menu for a
moment, but didn't really take anything in. My mind was
still on Priya and her family. "Trickery, then. No one likes
to be made a fool of, especially not by their nearest and
dearest. Priya's parents are going to be hurt."

He studied my face. "And you don't like it when people
get hurt, do you? You're very caring."

I shrugged. "I don't think I'm unusual in that. I can't
understand Priya's attitude. I know she loves her mum
and dad. Surely it would be better to tell the truth?"

"It's not always that simple. Love can come tied up
with so many obligations that it's hard to see a way out.
And some parents literally won't take no for an answer."

"But she's not a *child*," I said. "They can't force her to
get married if she doesn't want to."

He reached across the table for my hand and enclosed
it in his larger one. "She just wants them to be happy, and
this is her way of making them happy." He smiled, and his
dimple peeked out. "I'm not saying I think it's a great idea,
but she's a big girl. It's her decision." His thumb stroked
across the back of my hand, sending a tingle up my arm.

"Don't you worry about it. Your job is to eat way too much of this delicious food and have a fabulous time."

"I can probably manage that. And what's your job?"

"My job's easy. I just have to sit here and admire you."

I glanced down at the menu. "You're not going to help me eat way too much of the delicious food?"

"I reckon I can manage to multitask."

I snorted. "In my experience, men aren't usually that great at multitasking."

"Clearly you've been hanging out with some seriously sub-par guys." He grinned. "So now it's up to me to save the reputation of men everywhere."

That grin was infectious. "Behold me, ready to marvel at your skills."

"Fortunately, I love a challenge. And I also love Thai food. Let's order a selection and try them all."

After a bit of discussion we settled on our choices and he called the waiter over to take our order.

"You're serious about eating too much, aren't you?" I asked when he'd finished. "I'm going to explode if I eat even half that."

He lifted his glass in a toast. "Well, it was nice knowing you. Although, try not to. I'm not sure Maisie would forgive me if I killed you on our first proper date."

I took a sip of the wine. It was light and fruity with more than a hint of sweetness. I didn't know much about wines, but this one hit the spot.

"The Yule Ball was our first date," I reminded him.

He grimaced. "That doesn't really count. I ended up abandoning you and working instead."

I'd had plans to dance the night away in his arms, too. Still, it couldn't be helped. I liked that he'd been so quick to take charge and help, even though he'd been officially off duty. It showed that his job meant more to him than a pay cheque. He genuinely cared about our small community and its needs.

"I promise you I'm usually a better date than that," he added.

"Not a problem. It can be one of those funny stories—" I almost said, *that we can tell our grandkids*, but managed to stop myself just in time. Heat roared up my face and I ducked my head, taking another hasty sip of wine. What was I thinking? Not about marrying Curtis after half a date, that was for sure. It was just something that I used to say with Amy all the time. Thank goodness I'd caught myself. "—that everyone has," I finished lamely, hoping he hadn't noticed the flush. The lighting *was* pretty dim in here. I rubbed my neck, feeling like an awkward teenager.

"Just one of many for me," he said.

"Tell me one."

"What, and tarnish the good impression you have of me?" He laughed. "I'll leave those stories until you know me better."

We were still chatting when the food arrived. He was so easy to talk to, and seemed genuinely interested in everything I had to say, whether it was stories about Aunt Evie or discussions about setting up my business and all the clients I'd met so far. He listened without interrupting, waiting for me to finish before asking questions that took the conversation in new directions.

In short, he was a pleasure to be with, if a little reticent with stories of his own life. Oh, he spoke easily enough about his workmates and the challenges and curiosities of life as a policeman. He positively glowed when he talked about Maisie and the funny things she said and did. But he quickly changed the subject when I asked about his childhood, and neither of us mentioned the Kelly-shaped elephant in the room. I was quite sure he'd be as reluctant to discuss his previous relationship as I was.

The food was as delicious as promised, though I'd been right—we'd ordered far too much, even with Curtis's impressive ability to put it away. After a while, I had to slow down or burst.

Someone at Priya's table must have told a funny story, because they all broke into laughter. I looked across and saw Rakesh beaming, the centre of attention. Must have been him. He'd seemed a little shy when I'd met him, but I supposed with his own family he was much more relaxed.

Not that I really knew him. I grinned, recalling Priya's story about him stealing the toy car. He'd probably be horrified if he knew she'd told us.

"I was thinking about the Yule Ball," I said.

"Three out of ten, would not recommend," Curtis replied. "I promise I'll make it up to you."

I laughed. "No, not about us. About the theft."

"Ah." He put his chopsticks down—apparently there was a limit to how much he could eat after all—and wiped his mouth on his serviette. "I know that look. Are you going to solve this mystery, too? I swear, you're a better detective than any we have on the force. Not that I'm encouraging you, mind you. Police work is best left to the police."

"Yes, but you said yourself that the police are unlikely to find the necklace now. You searched Stellan, didn't you?"

He sipped his wine. "I did. Very thoroughly, too, before you ask, since he seemed the most likely suspect."

"What makes you say that?"

"Proximity, for one thing. He was closer than anyone except Geraldine and Jeff Borello. And Borello has been a pillar of the community as long as I can remember. Seems pretty unlikely he'd start a life of crime now."

"Anything else?" I was fishing to see if he had any inside information he'd share.

He shrugged. "Well, he *had* just committed to paying a crazy amount of money for that necklace. Too stupid—or stubborn—to stop when Phil Gottwig started pushing the bidding up. Maybe he decided he didn't want to pay it. He might not even have had that much to spare."

"I thought he was a rich architect with his own company?"

"The bank probably owns most of it."

I tapped my fingers on the table, thinking. "Priya said the same thing—that he might have had buyer's remorse. But I don't know. It was a charity event, after all. Everyone was there to bid up big and raise lots of money." I paused, chewing my lip. "So the police don't have any leads?"

"I haven't kept up with the investigation but I don't think so. We dusted the fuse box but couldn't get any usable prints off it."

I sighed. "That's a shame. If we could figure out who turned off the power, that would surely lead us to the thief."

"True. We're looking for at least two people."

"I thought I had it all figured out." I told him about my suspicions of Flick and Tim, and how that had led to nothing in the end. "Now I don't know where to start looking."

"You don't need to look," he said gently. "You don't have to solve everyone's problems."

"I have to solve this one."

"Why?"

"Aunt Evie."

He laughed. "Your aunt is certainly a force to be reckoned with. *I* wouldn't like to say no to her, either."

"You see my problem, then. I guess I'll just have to go through the photos I took when the lights came back on with a fine tooth comb and really study who's in the room." I'd already given them a cursory look, but I'd been focusing on Tim and Flick at the time. "Maybe that will turn up some leads. I might get Aunt Evie to help me, actually. She has lists of all the guests and which tables they were at."

"She'd know who everyone is."

I nodded. "Right. And then we can see if we can spot anyone who's missing."

"That only works if it was one of the guests. The thief might have had an accomplice who came in from outside just to turn off the power."

"Yeah." The lack of security on that staff entry at the

Metropole certainly made that a real possibility. "Did you pull the security footage from the car park?"

He groaned. "You know I shouldn't be sharing the details of an active investigation." He studied the last of his wine, swirling it around in the bottom of his glass. "Not that it's all that active. I think Delia's reached a dead-end."

I gave him my most winning smile. "So, did you?"

The dimple peeked out reluctantly. "That camera wasn't working. Hasn't been all year, apparently."

Another burst of laughter from Priya's table caught my attention. In the silence after it, I heard Amina ask Jack how he and Priya had met.

I looked at Jack, expecting a glib answer, but the pause lengthened. I froze, waiting for him to get his act together. Surely they went over their story, to make sure they were both on the same page? Had he forgotten? He cast an anguished glance at Priya, and all my anxiety about their deception came flooding back. They hadn't known each other long, so it was a stretch to think they could already be so attached. Would Amina realise the truth?

"We met at the hospital," Priya said, stepping into the silence with her usual calm confidence. "When Charlie was in hospital after her car accident."

My heart sank. No, no, no. Why did she say that? Jack hadn't moved in at that stage. As far as I knew, he'd still been in Brisbane. Sure, it made it seem as though they'd known each other longer, but it would be easy enough to disprove with only a little bit of detective work.

"Something wrong?" Curtis asked.

I shook my head. The question was, how likely was Amina to do that digging? If everything I'd heard about her was true, the chances seemed high. Priya may have just shot herself in the foot.

"Just getting distracted," I said, smiling at Curtis in apology. I was here with him, and he should be my focus. Not that focusing on Curtis was a hardship. But I'd be glad when the other party left. Priya might enjoy living on the edge, but it was bad for my digestion.

CHAPTER 16

PRIYA'S DIGESTION MUST HAVE BEEN MADE OF CAST IRON, because she was all smiles when I saw her the next morning.

Rufus and I had walked to the surf club café for a change of scene and to stretch our legs. I'd brought my laptop, but I hadn't fired it up when Priya turned up to grab a takeaway coffee and saw me there, gazing out at the ocean, lost in thought.

"I told you it would work," was the first thing out of her mouth as she plonked down in the seat opposite me and gave Rufus a cursory pat. "Did you see my mum last night? She was lapping it up."

"I can't believe you got away with it."

"Jack was amazing." Her eyes sparkled with delight. "What an absolute legend."

"He almost slipped up. I saw the look on his face when your mother asked how you'd met. And then *you* told her you met at the hospital two months ago." I waved my cake fork at her accusingly. "He hadn't even moved in then!"

She laughed. "My mother will never find that out."

I rolled my eyes. "Famous last words."

"Shut up and eat your cake."

I put the fork down. I'd ordered a slice of carrot cake with my coffee, not realising how generous the portions were, and I was struggling.

"I'm not really hungry."

"My, you're in a mood this morning. If you're not going to eat that …" She trailed off meaningfully, and I pushed the plate across the table towards her. She grabbed the teaspoon off my saucer and dug in. "Mmm. This is delicious." She waved the spoon at me. "I thought you'd be riding high after your date with Curtis."

I snorted. "Your table gave me indigestion."

"Oh, for goodness' sake. You're worse than Heidi. Relax! It was a triumph."

"So your parents bought it?"

"Mum asked Jack if he'd like to come to the temple with us next time we go. That's a sure sign that she liked him."

I raised an eyebrow. "Or that she wants to convert him to Hinduism so she can start planning your wedding."

Priya waved the cake fork airily. "He'll just be unavailable every time she asks. So sad, rostered on again. She'll forget all about it eventually."

That seemed highly unlikely, given what I knew of Amina. She was as determined as Aunt Evie and even more blunt, if that were possible. Something as dear to her as her only daughter's future happiness didn't seem like the kind of thing she'd simply forget about. But I took a sip of coffee and held my tongue. The family dinner had gone well, Priya was happy, and I was off the hook for being Amina's source of information on all things Jack. I wasn't going to spend another minute worrying about it.

Priya finished the cake and set the spoon down, ignoring the look of betrayal in Rufus's sorrowful brown eyes. She'd polished off the whole thing without recalling the starving dog waiting so patiently under the table for any stray crumbs to fall. In Rufus's eyes, making sure that there was a sufficient supply of stray crumbs was the main mission of anyone eating cake in his presence.

Well, of anyone eating anything, really, except lettuce. A dog had to have *some* standards. I reached down and stroked his soft ears until his eyes closed in bliss. Consolation pats made up for a lot.

"So," Priya said. "Tell me all about your date. You looked like you were having a good time."

"We were." I smiled at the memory. "Curtis is very easy to talk to."

"Not to mention easy on the eye." She took a sip of her coffee. "What's he like as a kisser?"

"What sort of a question is that? He's, um ... he's fine, I guess."

"Fine?" She regarded me in surprise. "Just fine?"

"Well, great, then. He's great."

Her eyes narrowed. "You haven't kissed him yet."

"I have! Well, not like, *kissing* kissing. We're always getting interrupted, or we're in a hurry. You know."

"I really don't. What was stopping you kissing him last night when he dropped you home? I assume he drove you?"

"Yes, he did. I just … never mind." The truth was that I'd chickened out at the last minute. In my defence, it had been years since I'd been on a first date. What was the protocol these days? Did it look like you were offering more than a kiss if you invited them inside? I was no innocent, but I also didn't want to rush things. I needed to be sure that I wasn't just reaching for the first guy that came along after Will, to be sure that what I felt for Curtis was real. I took a hasty sip of my coffee. "Let's talk about something else."

She studied my face for a moment, then smiled, obviously deciding—for once—not to push for answers.

"Sure. Did you tell him about my theory that Stellan may have walked out with the necklace in his underpants? What did he think?"

I laughed. "He quite likes Stellan as a suspect himself, but he thinks he would have found it when he patted him down. He was pretty thorough."

She looked unconvinced, so I reached for my laptop.

"I took a quick series of shots of the whole room as soon as the lights came back on. I thought I'd go through them again and see if I could spot anyone suspiciously out of place, or anyone missing who should have been there."

"Good idea." She tugged her chair around to the same side of the table as mine. Under the table, Rufus heaved a sigh at being disturbed and shifted his weight onto my feet. "I'll help you."

EMERALD FINN

I started up the laptop and brought up the photos from the ball, skimming through until I found the three I was talking about. I was rather proud of myself, actually, for thinking of it. All my hopes were pinned on finding a clue that would help me now, since otherwise I was pretty much out of ideas. I mean, Stellan may well have managed to sneak the necklace out in his jocks, despite Curtis's search, but I didn't see how I could ever prove that. Unless I could find something in these photos, my investigation was pretty much dead in the water, and I hated the thought of going to Aunt Evie with that news. She'd be so disappointed.

Priya leaned closer, her dark hair brushing my shoulder. "Nice clear shots. It's a bit dark, though, isn't it? I didn't realise on the night that the lighting was so dim. You can't really tell who's at those back tables."

"I can bring up the brightness on the images." I did that as I spoke, adjusting the contrast at the same time so everything didn't just blur into an over-exposed mess. "But I'm more interested in the people at the front tables and anyone standing or walking around. I don't think anyone down the back could have got there and back in time. So we can pretty much ignore anyone who's in their seats at the furthest tables."

"Someone at those tables could have gone to turn out the lights," she pointed out. "And there are a couple of gaps. Look at that one there."

I looked where she was pointing and laughed. "That's Delia's table. They're all police and their partners. I doubt we're going to find our criminal there."

"There's that waiter, the one who works at Mum's surgery. Patrick something. He's got a juvie record."

I studied Patrick's serious face. He looked bored out of his brain, still focused on the plates he was stacking on his arm, as if the lights going off and on again hadn't been enough to relieve the monotony of waiting tables at a large function.

"I already ruled him out. Your mum got all Mama Bear and ferocious that he'd even been suggested. And anyway, look at how far he is from the stage. He's right in the middle of the room, holding a stack of plates. There's no way he could have run to the stage, grabbed the necklace, and got back there and picked up all those plates in the dark."

She made a noncommittal noise, as if she didn't like to let go of the theory. "What about the cute bartender, then?" She pointed at Tim, close to Flick's table, with a dozen glasses stacked up one arm. "Or are you going to say he couldn't have picked up all those glasses in the dark, too?"

"I've already ruled him out, too, remember?"

"I know you said that, but couldn't he have done it anyway? Even if he *is* Flick's long-lost half-brother?"

I sighed. "I really don't know. I can't see why he would. It doesn't seem like the best way to endear yourself to your new family."

"Maybe he wanted it for himself. It was his dad, too. Or maybe he stole it so he could give it to her and earn himself some brownie points."

"How would he even know the necklace's history until

149

the auctioneer announced it? He would have had to come up with a plan on the spot to steal it. And even if he is some criminal mastermind who can hatch diabolical plans on the fly, who would be his accomplice? He's new in town and barely knows anyone. *Someone* had to turn off the lights."

"Could have been one of the other staff. He knows some of them."

I shook my head. "You're determined to make it him, aren't you? How long do you think you'd have to know someone to ask them to help you commit a crime and not have them either laugh in your face or turn you in to the police immediately?"

She pouted at me. "Fine. It wasn't him. But that's the question, isn't it? Who turned off the lights?"

"Yes." I scanned the photo, hoping that something would jump out at me. "Figuring that out would be a huge help."

"I suppose the police talked to all the kitchen staff and no one saw anyone near the fuse box?"

"Of course. And there's no surveillance footage from the car park camera, so anyone could have come in from outside to do it."

I clicked through to the next photo, which had Geraldine's table and half of ours in the foreground.

"Where's Stellan's wife?" Priya asked immediately, pointing at the two empty chairs where Stellan and his wife had been sitting.

"You can see her in the next photo," I said, clicking

150

through. "She's talking to someone at the table behind Aunt Evie."

Priya frowned. "Where?"

I pointed at the screen, where a woman in a black gown was standing with her back to the camera, talking to a young man whose bowtie was on crooked. Every time I looked at this photo my fingers itched to straighten it.

"That's not Stellan's wife," Priya said. "That's Rebecca Standish."

I peered at the screen. "Are you sure? I could have sworn his wife was wearing a dress just like that. And look at her hair."

"Nope." She shook her head decisively. "His wife's hair is much wavier than that. And she's not wearing a wedding ring—see there? Rebecca's not married."

"Wow." I sat back, flummoxed. Rufus shoved his wet nose into the palm of my hand, and I patted him absently. "I could have sworn that was Stellan's wife. What's her name?"

"Louisa."

"So he married the girl he stole from Phil?"

Priya snorted. "I don't think there was any stealing involved. I asked around after the ball and I heard she was making moves on Stellan before she and Phil even broke up."

"Can you see her anywhere?"

We both studied the photo. Where else would Louisa Eriksson be? I flicked back to the previous photo, but we both agreed there was no sign of her there. Nor could we find her in the other two snaps.

"She could have gone to the toilet," Priya said.

"In the middle of an auction where her husband was potentially spending thousands of dollars? I don't think so."

"Nature's call can be pretty urgent. Especially if you've drunk a lot of wine." But Priya's eyes were gleaming, her reporter's instincts aroused, and I knew she didn't believe that.

I grinned at her. "Or ... she might have disappeared downstairs to flick a switch."

CHAPTER 17

FOR THE REST OF THE AFTERNOON I WRESTLED WITH THE problem of how to find out where Louisa Eriksson had been. I often resorted to offering a free photo as an excuse to visit someone I didn't know. It was always easier to start a conversation when you began by giving a person something—it made people more receptive. But I was pretty sure that offering Stellan a photo of himself on stage with Geraldine in the moments before the necklace disappeared wouldn't put him in a receptive mood. Not only did he not get his necklace, but he was now the prime suspect in its disappearance.

In the end, I did what I probably should have done from the start, and rang Aunt Evie.

"How well do you know Stellan Eriksson?" I asked her.

"Well enough to say hello when I see him in the street. Not well enough to donate a kidney for him."

I laughed. "Let's hope he doesn't need a kidney donation, then."

"Why do you ask?"

"I want to know where Louisa was when the lights went out, because she wasn't in the ballroom when they came back on."

"Ooooh." I could picture Aunt Evie's eyes widening. Her next words were whispered. "How do you know?"

"Are you out somewhere? Is this a bad time?"

"No. I'm watching an old Doris Day movie."

"Then why are you whispering? Are you afraid Doris will hear you?"

"Don't be silly," she said briskly in her normal tone. "So how do you know she wasn't in the ballroom?"

"Remember those photos I took when the lights came back on? Priya and I have been over them and we can't see her anywhere."

"That seems odd. Especially when you consider her husband was bidding thousands of dollars for a necklace, presumably for her."

"That's exactly what I said!" I was pleased to have someone share my views. "You'd think she'd be glued to the action. Priya thought she might have gone to the bathroom."

"What rot! As if she couldn't hold it in for a momentous occasion like that. Even *I* could wait five minutes if someone was buying me a sapphire necklace, and my bladder must be thirty years older than hers."

"Right. And if she wasn't in the bathroom, where was she?"

"Are you thinking she might have been the one who flicked the switch?"

"I am indeed. That's why I was wondering if you knew Stellan well enough to give me an excuse to see him."

There was a short pause. "I suppose we could drop into his offices and say we were expressing our condolences on the loss of the necklace."

"It's not as if the necklace *died*." Although, if I got desperate enough, maybe I'd do just that.

"Hmmm. His house backs onto the national park. We could spy on them from the trees with binoculars."

"And what? See if they're tossing the necklace around the kitchen? I don't think so."

In fact, I didn't want Aunt Evie involved at all. She was all enthusiasm and very little discretion. She'd once suggested we break into a suspect's house and search it, which showed an admirable devotion to the cause, but a terrifying lack of regard for law and order.

"Well, then. I suppose you could make an appointment to see him in his official capacity."

"As an architect?"

"Why not? Tell him you want to build a pergola or something."

"But I'm renting!"

"So? *He* doesn't know that."

That stopped me. One thing you could say about Aunt Evie—she certainly had a lot of front. She would think nothing of marching into an architect's office and spinning him a story about her imaginary dream pergola. I squared my shoulders. If she could do it, I could, too.

I felt a little less confident the next morning. I rang the

offices of Eriksson and Arthur, and managed to convince the receptionist to slot me into Stellan's schedule.

"There," I said to Rufus. "All done. Now all I have to do is bring the conversation around to what I really want to talk about. Shouldn't be a problem, should it?"

Rufus was draped across my feet where I sat on the lounge. He thumped his tail lazily on the carpet, which I took to mean that he was confident there'd be no problem.

However, he was less encouraging a couple of hours later when he realised I intended to visit the offices of Eriksson and Arthur without him. I'd put on a pretty floral dress and a pair of red strappy sandals for the meeting. They weren't the kind of shoes for walking to town, even if I thought that a large and occasionally excitable dog would be welcome in an architect's office. Which I didn't.

He'd picked up on my getting ready signals and was waiting at the front door, wagging happily, when I came downstairs from my bedroom.

"Sorry, boy, you'll have to stay home."

The tail wag faltered and he gave me a look of such abject misery that I wavered. Maybe I could carry my sandals in a bag and change into them when I got there? It *was* only ten minutes' walk. It seemed silly to take the car.

I swore that dog had ESP. His tail wagged harder, as if he knew I was changing my mind. He gave a hopeful whine, and that sealed the deal.

"Fine. Wait here. I'll go grab my walking shoes."

I also grabbed a page I'd torn out of a magazine that showed a happy family lounging in their pergola, to show

Stellan what I had in mind. I presumed he'd expect me to have at least some idea of what I was asking for.

Rufus pranced happily ahead of me down the street, his tail held high like a victory plume. He carefully weed on each telegraph pole we passed, looking back at me each time to check I was keeping up. I was glad he'd managed to convince me to walk in the end—Sunny Bay had put on another glorious day, and at this time of the morning it wasn't yet too hot to enjoy a walk.

When we got into town I realised that Stellan's offices were upstairs, above a pizza place and a store that sold touristy knickknacks. Much to his disgust, I clipped Rufus's lead on and tied it firmly to a nearby pole in the shade.

"Wait here for me, boy. Sit. Good boy! This won't take long."

I slipped him a dog treat as I balanced on one leg, swapping my walking shoes for my sandals. He slobbered happily on my hand, which I wiped on my pants. Then I straightened the strap of my bag over my shoulder and climbed the stairs.

At the top I was greeted by a glass door, with *Erikkson and Arthur, Architects*, printed on it in a neat, black font. The hum of air-conditioning greeted me as I stepped inside.

"Hi," I said to the receptionist, a middle-aged woman with a friendly smile. "I'm Charlie Carter. I have an appointment to see Mr Erikkson."

"Take a seat, Miss Carter. He won't be long."

About ten minutes later, Stellan appeared, and I jumped up.

"Miss Carter? Come in, please."

I followed him into a small but neat office. Architectural drawings and blueprints were pinned on one wall. Behind his desk, a large window flooded the room with light. When I sat down in the chair facing it, I felt as if were under interrogation.

He must have noticed me squinting. "Would you like me to close the blind?"

"Oh! No, it's fine. It's a lovely day."

"It is," he agreed, but he pulled the blind down partway anyway, enough so that the sun wasn't hitting my face anymore. Then he seated himself behind the desk and smiled at me. "Now, what can I do for you?"

"I'm thinking of building a pergola in my backyard," I said.

His smile dimmed somewhat. "A pergola?"

"Yes." I fumbled in my bag and pulled out the picture, now a little crumpled. "Something like this one."

He took the picture from me and studied it a moment before passing it back. "You do realise that there are companies that specialise in building this kind of thing? You don't need an architect to design one for you."

"Really?" I widened my eyes, trying to look clueless and appealing. "I had no idea."

"I can give you the names of a couple in Newcastle, if you like."

"That would be marvellous. I'm so sorry to take up your time for nothing. You must have lots of important buildings to design." I didn't quite flutter my eyelashes, but he puffed out his chest a little, making the obvious connection between important buildings and his own importance as their architect.

You always caught more flies with honey than vinegar, as Aunt Evie liked to say. I was prepared to apply even more honey, hoping to put him in a receptive mood, but it turned out to be unnecessary.

"You know," he said, frowning slightly as he studied my face. "I can't get over the feeling that I know you. Have we met before?"

"Not precisely," I said, "but I was sitting on the next table over from yours at the Yule Ball." At the mention of the ball, his frown deepened. "And I was taking a photograph of you on the stage shaking hands with Geraldine when the lights went out."

"Ah. I thought I recognised you." His frown lingered as he neatened the papers on the desk in front of him. I could tell he was preparing to throw me out. Clearly he had no interest in discussing the Yule Ball.

"I was so sorry that happened," I said, smiling sweetly. "It was such a shame that you never got your necklace. Your wife must have been disappointed."

"Yes, she was a little." He pushed his chair back, preparing to rise.

I hurried on. "And she missed the end of the auction, too!"

He froze, his hands on the edge of the desk. "What do you mean?"

"You know—she wasn't in the room when you won

the auction. Such a shame for her to miss that big moment."

There was no expression in his face. "I'm sure you must be mistaken."

"Oh, no. It comes with being a photographer. I notice things. I thought it was odd, so I checked my photos, and she definitely wasn't in the room when the lights came back on."

He stared at me for a long moment. "She had to go to the bathroom."

"It must have been quite urgent."

He folded his arms tightly across his chest. "What are you implying, Miss Carter?"

"Nothing." I gave him my best innocent look, but he clearly wasn't buying it.

"Did Phil send you?"

"Phil Gottwig? No, of course not. Nobody sent me."

"Because if he thinks he can pin this on me, he'll be hearing from my lawyers. I've had quite enough of his antics."

"Truly, I've got nothing to do with Phil."

"Then I'll thank you to keep your accusations to yourself. If you really want to know who took that necklace, you should be looking at the waitstaff, not the guests."

Now it was my turn to frown. "Just because people buy a ticket to a ball, that automatically makes them honest people?" And the people who worked the ball were automatically dishonest?

"I already told the police, there's one waiter in particular they should be looking at, but would they listen to me?"

"You mean Patrick McGuigan? I can assure you, they've already looked at him quite enough. He's clean as a whistle. People need to stop assuming he's still the same guy he was years ago and let him get on with his life, instead of harassing him every time something happens. It's not right."

He shook his head impatiently. "Not him. Phil's kid. Ryan."

CHAPTER 18

I WAS WORKING ON MY WEBSITE, UPLOADING SOME RECENT photos, when the phone rang. I smiled when I saw Curtis's name pop up.

"Hi there," I said, the smile still evident in my voice.

His deep voice did delicious things to my insides, especially because I could tell that he was also smiling.

"Hi. How's my favourite photographer?"

"I bet you say that to all the photographers."

"Oh, sure. You're the third one this week."

"And it's only Monday."

"And it's only Monday," he agreed. "I'm fickle like that."

I laughed. "What are you doing?"

"Talking to my third-favourite photographer."

"Apart from that."

"Paperwork, mostly." He paused, and when he spoke again he sounded less sure of himself. "Listen, I was wondering if I could ask you a favour."

"Sure—unless you want me to bury a body for you. I'd have to be at least your second-favourite photographer for that. What's up?"

"It's a bit of an imposition. If you're too busy I understand completely—"

"Stop trying to talk me out of it before you've even asked me. What do you need?"

"I'm at work until five, and Mum was going to pick up Maisie for me and look after her until I got off work. But Mum's just rung to tell me she's got some kind of tummy bug so now I'm looking for someone else who could pick Maisie up from vacation care and look after her for a couple of hours."

"Wow, what a daunting task. No wonder you didn't want to ask me. Of course I'll do it. Maisie and I will have a blast." Already I was planning what we could get up to together to fill in a couple of hours. Eating fairy bread and playing with Rufus featured high on the list. "What time does she finish at vacation care?"

"Usually around three, but I can ask them to keep her longer if it's a problem."

"No problem at all."

"Thanks. I appreciate it."

"So *now* I'm your favourite photographer?"

"Top of the list!"

"Great. Then maybe you can tell me what you know about Ryan Gottwig."

"Ah ... remind me who Ryan Gottwig is?"

"Phil Gottwig's son. Apparently he was working as a waiter at the Yule Ball." Well, according to Stellan, anyway, and he could be lying to protect his wife. I'd checked my photos as soon as I'd got home from talking to him, but since I didn't know what Ryan looked like, I wasn't sure if he was in them or not. There was one waiter half-turned away from the camera who might have been a teenaged boy. I'd have to ask Aunt Evie. She'd be bound to know.

"Sorry to disappoint, but I don't know much about him, other than that he got a warning last year for getting caught at a party with a joint. Pretty sure he's still at school. Why?"

That was interesting. Maybe he needed money for drugs.

"I was talking to Stellan Eriksson this morning—"

He groaned. "Are you still trying to find that necklace?"

"Of course."

"I should have known."

"I was trying to find out where his wife was when the necklace disappeared. She wasn't in the ballroom, you know."

"And what did he say?"

"Well, obviously he wasn't going to admit that she was running around turning off switches. He said she was in the bathroom, and the police should be looking at Phil's son Ryan."

"You know there's a longstanding feud between Phil and Stellan, right? It doesn't surprise me that he'd be trying to pin the blame on a member of Phil's family. There's probably nothing more to it than that."

I got up and wandered into the kitchen, pacing restlessly. "Don't you think it's suspicious that Louisa Eriksson wasn't there to see her husband win the auction, though? Especially since he was bidding against Phil. Neither of them like Phil, so you'd think she'd be keen to see Stellan beat him."

The smile was back in his voice. "I can tell *you* think it's suspicious."

"I just can't figure out how Stellan could have got the necklace out of there without being caught."

"You know Stellan's been on the town council in the past? And his firm has made some sizeable donations to local causes. He's a pretty decent guy."

I sighed. "I can tell you're trying to talk me out of this theory."

"Well, I've been thinking about it, and I just don't think the timing works. If Stellan decided to steal the necklace instead of paying through the nose for it, he only had a very short time between the end of the auction and when he got up on stage to hatch the plan and send his wife off in search of the fuse box."

"Unless it was pre-planned," I said.

"What would be his motive, then?"

"Maybe just because he hates Phil? No, you're right, that doesn't make any sense. How would stealing the necklace hurt Phil?"

"Exactly."

"Well, maybe there *was* no accomplice. The circuit tripped all on its own, and Stellan just took advantage of the sudden blackout because he had buyer's remorse."

"The chances of it being a random circuit getting overloaded at exactly the right moment seem vanishingly small."

"Yeah. I guess I need to think about it some more."

"You do that," he said. "Anyway, I'll let vacation care know to expect you at three. Maisie will be so excited to see you. Thanks again, but I've got to get back to work. I'll come past just after five to pick her up."

"See you then."

Excited didn't do Maisie's reaction justice when I arrived to collect her later that afternoon.

"Charlie!" she shrieked, then hurtled towards me. She was only six, but if I hadn't been braced for impact she might have knocked me down with the force of her greeting. As she threw her arms around my waist I reflected that having Rufus was good practice for dealing with enthusiastic six-year-olds.

"Hi, Maisie Moo," I said, squeezing her back. "Are you ready to go?"

"Are *you* taking me home?" she asked, eyes wide.

"I'm taking you to *my* home," I said as I signed her out. "We're hanging out together until your dad is finished work."

"Can Rufus hang out with us too?"

"Sure. He's waiting for us outside. I tied him up to the railing."

That prompted another shriek of delight, and she towed me outside with great determination and a surprising amount of strength for such a small person. Rufus submitted to being hugged and kissed without protest, even delivering a kiss of his own.

Maisie's hand went to her cheek and she looked up at me, eyes shining. "He licked me."

"That's his way of saying he likes you."

"I like him, too." She took my hand as I shouldered her little backpack. "But I like you more."

"And I like you, so isn't that great? We all like each other." I grinned down at her as we set off along the street. The school, where the vacation care centre was, was in one of the back streets of Sunny Bay, and it was only a five-minute walk to my place.

"And you like my dad, too, don't you?"

Kids. Absolutely no filter. "Yep, I do. Tell me what you did today."

But she refused to be diverted. "He likes you, too. It took him ages to get ready to take you to the ball. He couldn't decide which shirt to wear. And he even went and got a haircut the day before."

"Uh-huh."

Curtis's hair was so short it would be hard to tell if he'd had a haircut. I certainly hadn't noticed.

"Are you going to marry him?"

I blinked. I wasn't even sure if Curtis had told her we were dating. "Heavens, Maisie, that's a funny question. Do you know who *you're* going to marry?"

"Oh, yes," she said at once. "I'm going to marry Tommy Cotton. He always has Tiny Teddies in his lunchbox."

Well, I'd heard of worse reasons to marry someone.

I was glad when we finally reached my house and I could distract her with food. I'd made some fairy bread before I'd left to pick her up and she fell on that as if she hadn't seen food in a week. Rufus positioned himself strategically beneath her chair, ready to catch anything that fell—or that she snuck to him. That dog was no fool.

"I'm going to a sleepover tonight," Maisie said as she munched. She had a milk moustache that was so adorable I couldn't bring myself to tell her to wipe her mouth.

"Really?" Six seemed young for sleepovers. "Who with?"

"It's my friend Bonnie's birthday. We're going to watch movies and stay up *all night*."

I grinned. I highly doubted that a bunch of six-year-olds would be able to stay awake all night, but I pitied Bonnie's poor mother as they made the attempt.

"I made Bonnie a card at care today. Do you want to see?"

"Of course."

She scrambled down from her seat and went to hunt around in her backpack. Rufus took the opportunity to clean up all the sprinkles that had fallen onto her chair in the meantime. He was thoughtful like that.

"This is it," she said, thrusting a folded piece of paper at me that was decorated with lots of sparkly heart stickers and a hand-drawn rainbow. One of the vacation care workers had printed *Happy birthday* in a curve above the rainbow.

"It's lovely," I said. "Bonnie's going to love it."

Maisie pulled her other hand out from behind her back. "And I made this for you."

It was a large bookmark made of bright red cardboard.

A photo of Maisie was glued to the top and the rest was decorated with stickers and wonky little hearts drawn in crayon. It was slightly creased from being in her bag.

"For me?" I asked. "Really?"

"Well, *really* we were supposed to make them for our mums. As a Christmas present." She looked down at her shoes. "But I told Mummy we were making them and she said she never read books so I needn't bother."

I almost gasped aloud. How could Kelly be so cruel? The poor little mite wanted to give her mum something special, and Kelly had knocked it back without a second thought.

Maisie looked up, her heart in her eyes. "But *you* like reading, don't you, Charlie?"

"I do," I said. "And it's the most beautiful bookmark I've ever seen. I'll treasure it forever."

"Really?" Her little face lit up. "It's not the best one," she confided. "Tommy's was better. He drew a reindeer on his."

"But this is from you, and that makes it very special to me." Just like it should have done to Kelly, if she hadn't been such a heartless monster. "Now every time I read a book, I'll think of you."

Maisie glowed with satisfaction. "*I* like books."

"I know you do."

"Are you going to give me a present, too?"

I laughed. "Yes, but you'll have to wait until Christmas."

She seemed satisfied with that, and we went out to play in the backyard with Rufus. Both Maisie and Rufus enjoyed tug-of-war, but Maisie wasn't heavy enough to beat him at that. So she switched to throwing a tennis ball for him, laughing every time as he tore off to grab the ball.

"You'll get sick of throwing it long before he gets sick of bringing it back," I said as Rufus dropped the slobbery ball at her feet again.

"Then I'll make it harder for him," Maisie said.

I snorted. Her throwing strength was about what you'd expect from a six-year-old, so Rufus wasn't exactly getting a workout running after the ball.

"How are you going to do that?"

"Like this." She feinted throwing the ball and Rufus hared off again. Maisie smirked at me as she dropped the ball into a pot full of geraniums. "Now he'll never find it."

We both laughed as Rufus zoomed back and forth across the yard, looking more and more confused as the ball failed to materialise. Eventually I plucked it out and threw it to him. He came trotting back with it and flopped at my feet, worn out from all that searching.

"He'd probably feel better if he had some ice cream," Maisie said, in the tone of an elder dispensing wisdom.

This child made me laugh so much it was hard to keep a straight face. "Do you think so?"

She nodded solemnly. "We'd feel better, too. It's very hot, isn't it?"

I took her not-at-all subtle hint and got us some ice cream. We'd finished it and were curled up on the couch watching kids' TV when Curtis arrived to pick her up.

"Hi," I said, a little overwhelmed at the reality of Curtis in his uniform. Obviously I didn't *forget* that he was a good-looking guy in between meetings, but somehow I got amazed all over again every time I saw him at just how attractive he was. He seemed bigger, brighter, just *more* somehow in person, as if I'd been looking at him in black and white and now I saw him in colour.

"Hi." He leaned in to brush my lips with a kiss that he broke off as Maisie appeared behind me with her backpack. "Thanks so much for doing this. I hope she wasn't any trouble?"

"Of course not. She's a delight. Aren't you, Maisie?"

She nodded. "Daddy, I played with Rufus and we had fairy bread and ice cream. Can we go now?"

He laughed. "You're in a hurry."

"It's Bonnie's party," she reminded him.

"So it is. Say goodbye to Charlie then, and thank her for having you."

She threw her arms around my waist in a quick hug.

"Bye, Charlie. Thanks," she muttered into my belly button, then looked up at her father expectantly.

He took her hand. "Looks like we're leaving."

"Would you like to join me for dinner?" I asked. "Once you get Maisie to her party? Jack and I often have pizza on his back deck on Mondays if he's not working. I think Priya's coming tonight, too."

He raised an eyebrow. "Taking their fake romance to the next level? I wouldn't miss it."

CHAPTER 19

I TIDIED UP AFTER THEY'D GONE, GATHERING CUPS AND PLATES from various places and stacking them on the sink. Looking out the kitchen window, I caught sight of the tennis ball and smiled, remembering Rufus's fruitless search. Maisie was a clever little thing.

I paused in the act of rinsing a plate. Such a cunning piece of misdirection. Could something like that have happened at the Yule Ball?

Everyone assumed that the thief had sneaked the necklace out of the ballroom—but what if they had hidden it somewhere instead? It made sense. They must have realised that as soon as people noticed that the necklace was gone, everyone would be searched—particularly those who were closest enough to be likely thieves, like Stellan. Sneaking it out *might* be possible, but it was risky. Hiding it somewhere and coming back for it later, when no one was watching, meant much less likelihood of being caught.

The problem was a lack of hiding places in the ball-room. The only things on the stage were the auctioneer's lectern and a stand where the auction items had been displayed. Nowhere there to hide something.

On the ballroom floor there were only tables and chairs. Under a tablecloth, perhaps? But when the waiters cleared the tables after the event, either someone would discover it or it would end up bundled in with the laundry and probably lost forever. The same went for dropping it in a half-full cup of coffee.

And then it hit me. The beautiful black vases full of flowers. The flowers were fake, so there was no water to be tipped out, and they belonged to the hotel. I was betting those arrangements got shoved in a cupboard somewhere until the next time they were needed.

"So all the thief has to do is wait for the fuss to die down, then come back and dig around in the bottom of a few vases until they find the right one," I said to Rufus.

He wagged at me a little doubtfully.

"You're right. Whoever the thief was, they've probably already been back and retrieved it. I'll never know if I was right. But just in case ..."

I grabbed my phone and rang the Metropole, praying I wasn't too late. It was after five; Greta had probably already left for the day. But when I asked to be put through to her, she answered after the first ring.

"Greta Chalmers, how can I help you?"

"Hi, Greta! It's Charlie Carter, the photographer."

"Hi, Charlie. What can I do for you?"

I scooped up my car keys and handbag as I spoke.

"You're probably just about to leave—I'm sorry to hold you up, but could you wait five minutes until I get there? I'm on my way."

"Of course," she said. "I won't be going anywhere for at least another hour. I have a big corporate function on Christmas Eve to prepare for. I hope there's nothing wrong?"

"Everything's fine," I assured her. "There's just something I need to see you in person about. I'll be there in five."

I made it in three, parked in the hotel car park and sprinted up the stairs. I already knew where Greta's office was, so I went straight there, even though the sign on that corridor said *Staff Only*.

I tapped on Greta's open office door.

"Hi." She stood up, smiling, and indicated her visitor's chair. "Would you like a seat?"

Now that I was here, I was jittery with excitement. "No, thanks. I won't take up much of your time. I have a theory I'd like to test."

"Oh? What kind of theory?"

"About what happened to the missing sapphire necklace."

"I'm all ears."

"It's probably a dumb idea, but I was wondering if the thief might have dropped the necklace into one of the table centrepieces, meaning to come back for it later when the heat had died down." I told her about Maisie "throwing" the ball for Rufus and how that bit of sneakiness had inspired me.

Her eyes gleamed. "That's not a dumb idea at all. The police were just like Rufus, running around searching everywhere they thought the necklace should be, while all the time it was hidden somewhere unexpected." She stood up and grabbed a heavy keyring from her desk drawer. "Let's go see."

I followed her from the room. "Has anyone else asked about the flower arrangements? Has anyone else been here?"

She threw me a grin over her shoulder. "No one has asked to see the flower arrangements that I know of. That would be a pretty weird request. But as to anyone being here—it's a hotel. There are people in and out of here all the time."

"But have you seen anyone in the staff areas who shouldn't be there?" I pressed.

She laughed. "Apart from you, you mean? No. No one. But that might just mean that the thief is biding their time, waiting for the uproar to die down."

She led me down a narrow staircase. Banging and clattering noises suggested we were getting close to the main kitchen.

"It's been almost a week since the ball. Surely they would have been back for the necklace by now? It's not as though the police have got the place cordoned off or anything." It was funny, but the closer I got to testing my theory, the less convincing I found it. "Have you used those vases since the Yule Ball?"

"No." She stopped in the service corridor and unlocked a door. When she switched on the light inside, the room proved to be a storage room. Half of it was taken up with audiovisual equipment, TVs, trolleys, and whiteboards. The opposite wall was covered in shelves, and various decorative pieces were stored there, including twenty black vases full of fake flowers. In between, spare dining chairs were stacked into unsteady towers. "The last wedding we had in supplied their own decorations. They were astonishing. Little battery-powered fountains in the middle of each table. I've never seen anything like it. Do you want to start on that shelf and I'll check this one?"

"Sure."

I moved to the other end of the cluttered room. I was taller than Greta, so she'd indicated I should search the vases on the upper shelf. I reached up and lifted down the first one. I pulled out the flowers with one hand, then tipped the vase with the other and gave it a little shake. A fake petal drifted down onto my feet.

No necklace. Undeterred, I shoved the flowers back in and reached for the next vase. Greta was moving faster than me. I realised that she wasn't bothering with tipping the vases upside down. All she did was pick each one up and give it a good shake before moving on to the next one.

I tried that with the next vase, though I couldn't help a certain reluctance. What if the necklace was caught around the flower stems, and it didn't rattle? We could pass right over it and never know. I chewed my lip, then tipped the flowers out anyway. I had to be sure.

Greta's next vase rattled when she shook it and we both stopped and stared at each other, transfixed.

"Ooh, what do we have here?" she asked.

"Don't just stand there," I begged. "What is it?"

She pulled the flowers out and tipped the vase upside down. The ring-pull off a can of soft drink fell into her hand.

She laughed. "Well, that certainly got my heart pumping. What a shame!"

She had reached the end of her shelf and I only had two vases left. It wasn't looking promising for my grand theory. I pulled out the next lot of flowers and tipped the vase over. It would have been so nice to find the necklace. If it had ever been here, the thief must have already retrieved it. More likely, someone had snuck it out in a hidden pocket—or even, as Priya had suggested, in their underwear. It would be easy enough to hide something that small in a bra, and no one would feel it through the padding.

I sighed as I started to shove the flowers back into the vase, then paused as a flash of something caught my eye under the harsh lightbulb that lit the small room. Excitement bubbling inside me, I put the vase back on the shelf, then spread the stems of the silk flowers apart.

There, twined around the base of a spray of leaves, was a gleaming sapphire necklace.

CHAPTER 20

I DROPPED INTO GRETA'S VISITOR'S CHAIR, MY KNEES STILL shaking with adrenaline. We stared at each other across her desk, grinning hugely. The sapphire necklace lay on the wooden surface between us.

"I still can't believe it was there," Greta said, shaking her head.

"Me neither."

"This calls for a celebration. I'll have the bar send up a bottle of champagne."

"I don't think I could drink right now." I couldn't stop looking at the beautiful blue stone, as if I were afraid it might disappear again if I took my eyes off it. "I already feel half drunk."

"Drunk on success." Greta laughed. "Never mind, I'll get you a bottle of champers anyway and you can take it with you."

"Oh, you don't need to do that," I said.

"It's the least we can do to thank you," she said firmly.

"You have no idea how embarrassing it was for the Metropole to have the necklace disappear on our watch. We're extremely grateful to you. Tell me again why you thought it might be there?"

I told her the story of Maisie and Rufus playing ball again. I'm sure she hadn't forgotten it in the short time since I'd told her earlier; she was just enjoying the moment.

"You're a regular Sherlock Holmes, aren't you?" she said admiringly when I was done. "It's a shame there's no way to know which table that particular vase was on. It would narrow down the list of suspects, wouldn't it? Who do you think dropped the necklace into that vase?"

I shrugged. "I guess anyone could have dropped it off at a random table as they passed, though it might have been tricky in the dark."

She looked disappointed, as if she'd expected me to solve the whole crime on the spot. "So it could have been anyone?"

"Who knows?" Privately I thought it was more likely that someone had rejoined their own table before discreetly slipping the sapphire into the vase once the uproar over the missing necklace was distracting everyone's attention. And Stellan would have been my main suspect, except that he'd been quite thoroughly searched before he'd left the stage.

There was still his suspiciously missing wife, though. I couldn't help thinking there must be *something* going on there, given how defensive Stellan had seemed when I'd asked where she was.

Could Stellan possibly have put it in his *mouth* to hide it from Curtis's search? Could he have tucked it into his cheek and still managed to talk? That was something I hadn't considered, though it seemed fraught with peril. Imagine if someone thumped you on the back and you accidentally swallowed it! You'd be conducting some very nasty searches for the next few days until it reappeared.

"What does Ryan Gottwig look like?" I asked, remembering my other suspect.

Her eyes widened. "Do you think it's *him*?"

"No, of course not," I said hurriedly. Maybe he *was* involved, but I didn't want to start any rumours. He was just a kid. "I took some photos as soon as the lights came back on, and I'm just checking everyone off, trying to figure out if anyone's missing. But I don't know what he looks like."

"He's tall and skinny," Greta said. "All elbows and knees, like a lot of teens before they fill out. He's got that lean runner's build—which isn't surprising, since he seems to take out most of the medals in his age group at every school athletics carnival."

"So, he's a runner?"

"Runner, long jumper, high jump star, you name it."

"And he was definitely working at the Yule Ball?"

"I'm sure he was."

"Okay, thanks." That was interesting. The waiter I'd thought might be Ryan was quite small. So Ryan the track star hadn't been in the ballroom when the lights came back on. He could have been in the kitchen, of course, but perhaps he'd been putting those long legs to good use running down the stairs to the fuse box.

"Well, I suppose I'd better make a few phone calls," Greta said.

The first one, as promised, was to the bar, and a woman in a waitress uniform turned up a few minutes later with a bottle of French champagne. Sacre bleu! The Metropole was spoiling me. The woman's eyes widened when she saw the necklace on the desk, and I figured news of our discovery would be all over the hotel before I left this room.

The next one was to the police, who promised to send someone around right away. Greta made us both a cup of tea and we chatted while we waited, the necklace lying between us on Greta's desk.

"Now I feel bad about touching it," I said. "We've probably left our fingerprints all over it."

"I don't think something like that would take finger-prints very well," Greta said. "It's probably fine."

This was confirmed by Officer Salerno, an older man with a kind smile, who arrived a few minutes later with his quiet young partner. I recognised them both from the ball.

"I should have known you'd be involved," he said to me once we'd explained our find. "Are you trying to do us out of our jobs?"

But he laughed, so I knew he was joking. I said sorry anyway.

"Don't be sorry. In most of these cases, the stolen items are never recovered, so this is a great outcome."

"What happens now?" Greta asked.

"Well, that depends on what Mrs Winderbaum wants us to do. If she wants us to continue with the investigation, we'll keep it as evidence. Otherwise, she can have it back."

"I was just about to ring her," Greta said. "We can ask." She dialled the number and put it on loudspeaker.

"Geraldine Winderbaum."

"Hello, Mrs Winderbaum, it's Greta Chalmers from the Metropole here. I have Charlie Carter and two lovely police officers with me, and we have some good news for you."

"Hello, Greta," Geraldine said. "I'm always happy to hear good news. What is it?"

"We've just found your missing necklace."

"That *is* good news. How marvellous! Where was it?"

Greta recounted our detective work, grinning at me the whole time. "Officer Salerno has a question for you."

"Yes." He cleared his throat and leaned closer to the phone. "Hello, Mrs Winderbaum. Do you want us to keep the investigation open?"

"Of course," she said. "I want to know who took it!"

"Okay. So we'll be taking the necklace into evidence."

"Oh, wait. You would have to keep it?"

"Of course. Can't really charge someone with a crime if you don't have the evidence, can you?" He chuckled.

"And how long would you keep it for?"

"That depends on how long it takes to find the thief. I have to warn you, it could be quite a long time."

There was a pause while Geraldine considered that. "Has Stellan paid for it yet, Greta?"

Greta glanced uncertainly at me.

"No," I said. "And I doubt he will until the investigation is finished. Who wants to pay for a necklace they can't have?"

Geraldine sighed. "You'd better drop the investigation, then."

"You're sure?" Officer Salerno asked, rocking back on his heels.

"The whole point was to raise money for the hospital, wasn't it? They need the money now, not in a few months or years, or however long it takes you to find the thief."

He nodded. "In that case, we'll bring the necklace around to you now."

"I'm actually in Sydney at the moment, and I won't be back until tomorrow morning."

"Is there someone home we can leave it with? Your daughter, perhaps?"

"Heavens, no." She sounded horrified. I guessed she was in enough trouble with Flick already over Tim. She didn't want to be flaunting the necklace she'd given away in Flick's face as well. "Just leave it at the Metropole until I get back."

"Actually, the Metropole would prefer someone else to take responsibility for it," Greta said quickly.

"I suppose you would, since you've lost it once already. Fine, then. Give it to Evelyn. It was in her safe for a couple of nights before the auction. It can stay there until Stellan pays and the committee hands it over."

"That would be Evie Labrecque?" Officer Salerno asked.

"Yes."

Greta ended the call soon after, and the police left with the necklace. Aunt Evie would be *so* excited when she saw them. I stood up to go, too.

"Don't forget your champagne," Greta said. "You've earned it!"

CHAPTER 21

Everyone had champagne on the brain tonight. Aunt Evie squealed like a little kid—Maisie would have been proud —when I walked into her villa a little later. The police had only just left and she was still holding the necklace.

"You found it! I always knew you would!" She caught my face between her hands and planted a smacking kiss on my lips, though she had to stand on tiptoe to do it. "This calls for champagne!"

"I have some in the car," I protested. "I don't need any more."

"Never mind *you*!" She marched into the kitchen, set the necklace down on the table, and took a bottle out of the fridge. "*I* need some. You have no idea how worried I've been about this."

"Why do you even have a bottle of champagne in the fridge?"

"It was a Christmas present. I got it in the Secret Santa at the ladies' luncheon last Friday." She peeled the foil off the top of the bottle, unwound the wire cage, and expertly twisted the cork out with only the slightest pop of release. "And now I have something to celebrate."

She poured two glasses and offered me one, holding her own out in a toast. "To my favourite niece!"

I lifted my own glass in response, smiling. "I'm your only niece."

"Doesn't matter." She swallowed half her champagne in one gulp, then started dancing around the kitchen. "You're still my favourite, you clever, clever thing. Now tell me all about it."

She drank the rest of her glass and filled it back up again while I gave her a rundown of my thinking and the search that Greta and I had undertaken. "Geraldine thought you wouldn't mind keeping it in your safe until Stellan paid up and ownership can be transferred to him."

"Fine, fine," she said. Clearly nothing was going to ruin her good mood now the necklace had been found. I knew she'd been worried about it, but I hadn't realised quite how stressed she'd been. "Although it might have been better to leave it where it was and stake out that storage room so we could catch the thief when they came to reclaim it."

I laughed. "I don't think the Metropole cares about it enough to institute a twenty-four hour watch on their storage room."

She waved the hand holding her drink impatiently, making the champagne slosh rather alarmingly around in the glass. "Not them. The police."

"Well, Geraldine told them to drop the case, so I don't

think they care. They're busy with other things at this time of year, anyway."

Aunt Evie made a little huffy noise. "Like going to Christmas parties."

"Like policing all the people getting drunk at Christmas parties and trying to keep the holiday road toll down." I took a sip of my champagne. "And maybe going to Christmas parties. But it's not as though the Crown jewels went missing, is it? I'm sure they think all's well that ends well, and that's one more thing off their plate."

"I wonder why the thief hasn't been back yet."

"Perhaps they have. Maybe they didn't realise the vases were stored in a locked room, and they couldn't get in."

She didn't look entirely convinced. "Surely someone with enough front to pull off a heist under the noses of nearly two hundred people wouldn't be above a little lock picking. Or bribing a staff member to unlock a door for them."

"Might be a little hard to explain why they wanted that particular door unlocked."

"Make it a big enough bribe and no explanations would be necessary."

I swirled the last of my champagne in the bottom of my glass. "I guess we'll never know now. The main thing is that we've got the necklace back. That's all that matters."

Aunt Evie tipped the bottle towards me. "Top up?"

"No more for me, thanks." I looked at my watch and

squeaked. "I've really got to run. I should have been home ten minutes ago. Curtis is coming over."

"In that case, don't let me keep you."

"You will put that in the safe straight away, won't you?" I took one last look at the glorious blue sapphire, set among its twinkling diamonds. It had caused so much trouble, but thank goodness that was all over now.

"Of course." Aunt Evie set her glass down and scooped up the necklace. "I'll do it right now."

She had a safe set into the concrete floor of her garage, hidden under a stack of cardboard boxes that held all her Christmas decorations. No one would ever know it was there.

I gave her a quick hug goodbye and hurried out to my car. It was less than five minutes to my house, but I was already late. It would be so embarrassing if Curtis turned up and I wasn't even home. I sent him a quick text before I started the car: *On my way.* There was no reply. Hopefully that meant that he was still in transit.

But when I pulled into my driveway, his car was already sitting outside, though there was no sign of him. I let myself in, fending off Rufus's exuberant greeting, and threw my handbag down on the couch.

A burst of masculine laughter from next door drew me to the kitchen window. Curtis and Jack were out on Jack's deck, beers in hand. I waved, but they were too engrossed in their conversation to notice me.

"Time for dinner," I told Rufus, and quickly got his food ready. He fell on it as though he hadn't seen food in a year, of course. He could always be relied on to eat quickly.

While he ate I grabbed out the bowl of salad I'd prepared earlier and the bottle of champagne Greta had given me.

Rufus went to the back door when he was done and looked meaningfully over his shoulder at me.

"Hold your horses," I said. "I'm coming."

The men looked over at the sound of the glass door sliding open. I stepped out on Rufus's heels and gave Curtis a rather sheepish smile.

"Sorry I wasn't home when you got here."

He smiled back. "I figured when you didn't answer the door that you must already be at Jack's, so I wandered over."

"I've been plying him with alcohol and regaling him with horror stories from the ward," Jack said cheerfully.

Curtis grinned. "Remind me never to let this guy change my bandages. He sounds like a monster."

"I'll be there in a sec," I said. "I just want to get changed first."

"You look fine to me," Jack said.

"More than fine," Curtis added.

"*Fine* isn't going to cut it when Priya turns up looking like a supermodel," I pointed out.

"Are you bringing Rufus?" Jack asked hopefully.

Jack adored dogs, but Sherlock didn't feel the same, so his dog opportunities were limited. But Sherlock spent most of the time when people were visiting sulking in the bedroom anyway, so, at Jack's urging, I'd been bringing Rufus along to our Monday nights on the deck.

"That depends on whether he's ready when I am." I shook a warning finger at Rufus, who was wandering around the yard as if he had all the time in the world. "You'd better poop fast, mister, if you want to come to Uncle Jack's, or you'll be left behind."

"You can't pressure a man into pooping before he's ready," Jack objected. "You'll give him constipation."

"That word isn't in this dog's vocabulary," I said. "He's a pooping machine."

I headed inside to change into jeans and a silky black top. Pizza at Jack's was a very casual affair, but I put on some lipstick, brushed my hair, and added some dangling silver earrings. I'd been kidding when I said I had to dress up because Priya would—really I wanted to look my best for Curtis. One day, if our relationship lasted that long, I'd be parading in front of him in holey T-shirts and baggy trackpants, but that day was not today.

Rufus and I arrived next door at the same time as Priya. She was also wearing jeans, with a white embroidered top that looked dynamite next to her warm brown skin, and carrying a box with the distinctive logo of Jenny's Bakery.

"Ooh, what's that?" I asked.

"Nice to see you, too," she said, grinning.

"Food first, friends after," I said firmly.

"It's a blueberry cheesecake."

"Yum." I nodded at Jack's front door, my hands full of salad and champagne. "He's left it unlocked. Would you?"

She opened it and we went through to the deck, Rufus trotting at our heels. Usually Jack spent five minutes greeting the dog before he got to me, but I noticed his attention turned first to Priya. He was effusive in his thanks for the cheesecake, and complimented her on everything from her shirt to her hair and her earrings before he even noticed that Rufus was there.

Not that Rufus cared. Jack was one of his favourite people, but Jack's yard was also full of good sniffs to be sniffed, and a dog had to prioritise. For once, Sherlock had deigned to join us instead of hiding upstairs. He was perched on the wooden railing of the deck, and he watched Rufus lope around the yard with his usual disdain.

I put my salad down on Jack's outdoor table.

"I keep telling you, you don't need to bring a salad," he said when he dragged himself away from Priya. "Pizza is a meal all by itself."

"Steady on there," Curtis said. "Pizza needs beer."

"Okay, sure. Pizza *and beer* is a meal all by itself. No one needs rabbit food, too."

"That rabbit food might just save your arteries from clogging up," Priya said.

"My arteries live for pizza. They spit in the face of cholesterol. They're manly arteries." He grinned at me. "Besides, the original point of pizza night was to save either of us cooking."

"Chopping up a few salad veggies doesn't count as cooking," I said. "Do you want to chill this champagne down or shall we open it right away?"

He picked up the bottle. "It's pretty cold."

"They probably had it in the fridge at the Metropole, but it's been in my car for half an hour."

Curtis had been watching me, that slow, sweet smile

of his lighting his face. "Why champagne? Are we celebrating something?"

"Nearly being finished work for Christmas," Priya said. "We shut for two whole weeks over Christmas and I can't wait."

"I wish I could say the same," Jack said, "but sadly people don't stop getting sick and needing operations because it's Christmas."

"Well, we're not celebrating that anyway," I said, smiling.

"Oh, check that smile," Priya said. "Have you got some good news?"

"You could say that." Happiness bubbled inside me. "Guys, you're not going to believe it. I found the necklace."

The three of them exchanged incredulous looks.

"Geraldine Winderbaum's necklace?" Priya's eyes were wide. "You *found* it?"

I laughed. "A little less shock and a little more admiration for my sleuthing talents might be nice. You're supposed to be impressed!"

"I'm *very* impressed," Curtis said. "Dumbfounded, actually."

"And?"

"And what?"

"And how much do you admire my sleuthing talents?"

That delicious dimple peeped out as he grinned. "Enormously. Stupendously."

"We bow before your greatness," Jack added. "How's that?"

"Pretty good, actually. Now, if only there was some actual bowing going on ..."

Priya rolled her eyes. "Just open the champagne already and give the woman a glass before her head explodes."

Jack obliged, shooting the cork across the back yard, much to Rufus's surprise. He came wagging up to us, drawn by the laughter and air of excitement. In his experience, such things usually led to treats for good dogs—or at least pats. He noticed Sherlock on the railing for the first time, and wagged harder, hopeful of making a friend. Sherlock gazed down on him with what looked a lot like contempt, but perhaps that was the cat's natural expression.

While Jack poured champagne for everyone, Curtis crouched down to scritch behind Rufus's ears. He looked up at me, which was a novel experience. It wasn't often I found myself taller than Curtis. The view was just as good from above as it was from below.

"If your ego has been sufficiently stroked, maybe you could tell us how you found it."

"Yes!" Priya's eyes lit up. She always loved a good story. "Let's hear the tale of your derring-do."

"Did you do some derring-do?" Jack asked, handing me a glass. "So you derring did?"

Priya thumped him playfully on the shoulder as I launched into the tale. After that the conversation naturally moved on to speculation on the identity of the thief, and why they hadn't come back for the necklace. Jack favoured the theory that they hadn't been able to get into the storeroom, whereas Priya decided they must have met with an accident. Curtis said nothing, merely watching us with amusement.

Finally, Jack remembered that we were supposed to be eating pizza and put in the order for delivery. Rufus, of course, begged shamelessly while we ate it, and didn't budge until I proved to him that it was all gone by showing him the empty boxes.

I thought I'd never be able to fit in any of Priya's cheesecake after all that pizza, but it turned out that I could, though I did feel extremely full afterwards. We settled into a lazy, comfortable circle once dinner was over, Curtis and I on the two-seater, me with my legs propped in his lap, and Priya and Jack opposite us, their chairs drawn close together. Rufus had clearly worn himself out with begging. He was sacked out on the deck between us, his paws twitching occasionally. Maybe he was dreaming of chasing Sherlock. Much to my surprise, Sherlock eventually wandered over and curled up next to him, using his back as a chin rest.

"Aww, that's so sweet," Jack said. "They're friends!"

"Only because Rufus is unconscious," I pointed out. "I don't think Sherlock likes him all that much when he's awake."

The talk settled into long, rambling stories and silly word games. All the champagne had made me sleepy, but I was having too much fun to want to think about going home. Curtis's hand lazily stroked my leg as Priya told some long, complicated story that had us all in stitches.

I almost didn't check my phone when it buzzed. It was

probably just a social media notification, and I was comfortable. I didn't know what made me change my mind, but I pulled it out of my pocket, still laughing.

I slammed my feet to the deck and leapt up, sobering as abruptly as if someone had poured a bucket of cold water over my head.

Curtis looked up at me in alarm. "What's wrong?"

"It's a text from Aunt Evie. She's in trouble." I held the phone out so he could see her message.

Two words: *coconut coconut.*

CHAPTER 22

Curtis took charge immediately. "We'll take my car."

I nodded, only stopping long enough to slide my feet back into my shoes.

"Wait for me!" Jack demanded. "I'm coming, too."

"You're drunk," Curtis said dismissively.

"Not *that* drunk."

"Well, I'm not staying behind by myself," Priya said.

Curtis opened his mouth to argue, then shook his head. "Fine. Let's not waste any time."

In less than thirty seconds we were on our way, his big four-wheel drive speeding through the dark streets of Sunrise Bay. He called the station and asked them to dispatch a car to meet us there.

"What's the problem?"

"Possible break and enter," he said, then hung up.

I glanced at his profile in the dark. There was a grim set to his jaw; he remembered that conversation at the ball, too.

"Do you think she's all right?" I asked. My heart was pounding like a jackhammer and I'd broken out into a cold sweat.

"We'll be there in two minutes," he said.

I nodded. He didn't know any more than I did what we'd find when we got there. I appreciated that he didn't try to soothe me with empty reassurances. He was worried, too.

"What was in that text?" Priya asked. She and Jack were in the back, and I noticed that she had Jack's hand in a tight grip.

"Remember at the ball, when Aunt Evie said if she were being held hostage, she'd post *coconut coconut* on social media so people would know she was under duress?"

Jack looked confused. "She's being held hostage?"

"I doubt it. But something's going on and she's not free to speak normally. There might be—there might be an intruder."

Curtis reached across to squeeze my hand, then glanced at Jack in the rear vision mirror.

"When we get there, you two go around to the back. Charlie, you've got a key, I assume?"

"Yes."

"Okay, you open the door, if it's not already open, and I'll go straight in."

"*We'll* go straight in."

His eyes were kind, but he had his professional face on. "You should wait outside for the patrol car. It could be dangerous."

"It's *my* aunt in there. I'm not waiting outside."

He sighed, as if he'd expected resistance. "Then stay behind me and don't get in my way. Jack, if I flush anyone out the back, it's up to you to grab them until I can get there."

"Will do."

The car turned into the grand entry of Sunrise Lodge, the name on the wall illuminated by floodlights. Street lights lit the narrow roads inside the village, but most of the homes were dark at this time of night. Curtis drove straight to Aunt Evie's villa and pulled into the driveway. Everything was dark, inside and out.

"Everyone ready? Let's go."

Jack and Priya ran for the side gate and disappeared into the darkness at the side of the villa. I leapt out of the car, keys already in my hand, and rushed to the front door.

"It's locked," I whispered.

Curtis nodded, looming at my back while I turned the key. But as I went to open the door, he pushed me gently but firmly aside and went in first.

He flicked on the lights in the entryway.

"Police!" he shouted. "Freeze!"

I craned to see around him, but the entry hall was small and Curtis was large. He turned on the lounge room light but no one was there, so we continued down the hall.

A figure dressed in dark clothes burst out of the second bedroom and sprinted for the kitchen. Curtis took off, shouting for him to stop, but the man was a lot closer than we were to the exit. By the time Curtis caught up, he'd already flung open the back door and gone.

There was a shout from outside, but I didn't follow Curtis out to see what had happened. I was more concerned about Aunt Evie. I hurried into the second bedroom, where the intruder had come from, but it was empty. She wasn't in her own bedroom, either, or in her tiny en-suite bathroom.

Increasingly worried, I checked the main bathroom. It wasn't a large villa—there were only the two bedrooms, two bathrooms, the kitchen, lounge room, and a tiny laundry, barely big enough for the washing machine and dryer. Certainly not large enough to conceal my missing aunt.

"Aunt Evie!" I shouted, panic making my voice shrill. "Where are you?"

"Charlie?" a muffled voice answered. "In here."

I ran back to Aunt Evie's bedroom in time to see her emerge from the closet, wearing a bright red pair of Christmas pyjamas. Her hair was mussed from hiding behind her winter coats, but otherwise she appeared unharmed.

I threw my arms around her. "Are you okay? Are you hurt?"

She hugged me back fiercely. "I'm all right. Just a little shaken."

"You need to sit down." I led her to the bed and she more or less collapsed onto it. I sat down beside her, still keeping my arm around her, more conscious than ever of how thin her shoulders were, how slight her form. She was shaking as I pressed a kiss to her temple.

"Was that Curtis I heard? Good of you to bring the cavalry." She glanced up at me with an attempt at her usual mischief. "I hope I didn't interrupt anything too steamy."

I rolled my eyes. "Jack and Priya are here, too."

"Really? Where's my dressing gown?"

"What? You don't want them to see your *Ho ho ho* pyjamas?"

She flapped her hands at me impatiently. "I have *guests*. Go and put the kettle on."

I left her primping her hair in the bathroom mirror and went to flick the kettle on. Outside, the lights in the tiny backyard were blazing and Priya was fussing over Jack, who was seated in one of the outdoor chairs.

I went to the back door. "What happened? Is Jack all right? Where's Curtis?"

There was a scrape on Jack's cheek, and another down his right arm.

"The guy came rushing out," Priya said. "Jack tried to grapple him, but he knocked him down and kept going. Curtis went after him. Is Evie okay?"

"Yes, just a little shaken. Why don't you come inside and I'll get out the first aid kit. I'm sure Aunt Evie's got some bandages and antiseptic for those grazes."

"If only I'd been a footballer," Jack said mournfully. "But all I ever played was basketball."

"It wouldn't have mattered," Priya said as she helped him out of the chair. He was a bit wobbly on his feet, which probably had more to do with the amount of beer he'd drunk tonight than his tussle with the intruder. "That guy was way heavier than you. He knocked you down without even breaking his stride."

The side gate clanged open and Curtis strode back into the yard, breathing heavily.

"What happened?" Priya asked.

"Lost him. He had a car waiting around the corner." He glanced at Jack. "Are you okay?"

"Fine." Jack looked rueful. "If you hadn't stopped to make sure I was all right, you probably would have caught him."

Curtis shrugged, then looked at me. "How's Evie?"

"She's fine."

His expression cleared. "That's the main thing."

"Let's go inside. I'm making tea."

We all went inside and I got the first aid kit out of the cupboard in the laundry for Jack. Priya helped him wash his grazes, then dabbed antiseptic on them. When he flinched, she told him sternly not to be a baby.

Aunt Evie swept in while this was going on, wearing a satin dressing gown and jewelled sandals. She'd smoothed her hair into its usual sleek style. If it wasn't for the fact that she still looked pale, you'd never know anything had happened to disturb her.

She glanced at the clock on the oven. "Well, isn't this fun! Another few minutes and we can have a midnight feast."

Curtis pulled out a chair for her at the kitchen table and fussed over her as she settled in it. Opposite her, Jack was still wincing and flinching as Priya ministered to him.

I set a cup of tea in front of her and slid into the seat next to her. "Can you tell us what happened?"

She took a sip of tea and I saw that her hands had

stopped shaking. Our company was restoring her to her usual self.

"I was in bed, trying to get comfy. I was having trouble sleeping. And I thought I heard the sound of the patio door sliding open. I thought perhaps I'd nodded off for a moment and imagined it, but then I heard someone moving around in the kitchen. A tiny bit of light was coming into my room, as if someone was out there with a torch."

"You must have been scared," Priya said.

"I was. I thought about lying very still and pretending to be asleep. And then I thought maybe I should get out of the house and call the police. My phone was on the bedside table, but I didn't want to call someone while I was still inside, in case whoever was in the kitchen heard me and it made it all worse. I was heading for the bedroom door when I realised the person was coming towards me."

"What did you do?" Jack's eyes were round.

Aunt Evie smiled at me. "I didn't have time for a long text explaining the situation, but I remembered our conversation at the ball, about what we'd do if we were ever being held hostage, and I thought, well, this is almost the same thing. So I dived into the wardrobe and hid behind the clothes and texted you." Her smile swept the room, taking in all four of us. "And you all came to my rescue."

I frowned. "It's awfully suspicious that someone breaks into your house the same night that I bring you that dratted sapphire necklace."

"But no one knows it's here except us," Aunt Evie objected. "And Greta, I suppose."

"And Geraldine," I said.

"It's not as though she's going to steal her own necklace, though, is it? And Greta could have offered to keep it at the Metropole if she'd wanted to steal it. No need to break in here."

"That definitely wasn't any Geraldine that knocked me down," Jack said. "That was a bloke."

"So you didn't see the intruder at all?" Curtis asked.

Aunt Evie shook her head.

"Don't look at me," Jack said. "All I saw was a guy in black clothing, and then I was facedown on the pavers."

"And I only saw him from the back," Curtis said.

"He was wearing a balaclava anyway," Priya said. "He was a pretty solid guy, but I only saw him for a second."

So not Ryan, if Greta was right about Ryan being tall and gangly. Maybe Tim?

"Where's that patrol car?" Curtis said. "We could at least try to get some fingerprints."

"Never mind fingerprints," Priya said. "What about the necklace? Did he get it?"

"I shouldn't think so," Aunt Evie said. "It's in the safe."

"Perhaps you should check."

She gave me an uncertain look, then got up and headed for the garage. I followed her, Curtis on my heels, and after a moment, Priya and Jack came too. Just as well Aunt Evie's convertible wasn't too big, because there wasn't much space with all of us in there.

I helped Aunt Evie shift the boxes, which were empty

at this time of year since all her Christmas decorations were up, revealing the safe set into the concrete floor. Aunt Evie groaned as she knelt down and reached for the keypad.

She paused and looked up at all of us crowding around. "Now you're all going to know the combination."

"We'll look away," Priya said, and the three of them did. I already knew the combination so I watched as she opened the safe and drew out a red velvet jewellery box.

"You can look now," Aunt Evie said as she opened the box. A strand of pearls shone softly inside, and cuddled up to the pearls was the sapphire necklace. "See? All safe and sound."

"Thank goodness," I said.

"It's a pretty thing, isn't it?" Aunt Evie pulled the necklace out, letting it dangle from her fingers and catch the light as the sapphire slowly turned. "Oh, my knees. I'm too old for this."

She struggled to stand up. I reached to help her, but I was too late. She wobbled and flung out a hand to catch herself.

The sapphire hit the brick wall and smashed.

CHAPTER 23

FOR A MOMENT, WE STOOD, FROZEN.

"Oh, my," Aunt Evie said.

"That's not good," Priya said.

Curtis said nothing, merely crouched down to examine the blue shards on the floor. Then he stood up and placed his foot deliberately on one of them. From underneath his shoe came a crunching sound that made me wince.

"Glass," he said.

Aunt Evie continued to stare at the floor, completely flummoxed. "But ... But ..."

Jack shook his head. "I don't understand. How could the thief have switched necklaces?"

Priya gave him an impatient look. "You *have* had a lot to drink, haven't you? No one switched necklaces. The necklace was a fake to begin with."

Aunt Evie looked pained. "I don't suppose there could be some ... mix-up, could there?"

I closed my eyes for a moment. I understood her ...

what would you call it? Hurt? Confusion? We'd been swindled. I felt an echo of it myself. To think I'd spent all this time and effort running around trying to locate a necklace that wasn't even real.

"There's no mix-up. I found this in one of the vases that were used on the tables the night of the ball. This is the necklace that was auctioned off and then stolen that night." I met her disappointed gaze. "This is the necklace that Geraldine donated."

The tiny blue shards of glass winked in the light. She nudged them with her toe and huffed out a sigh. "The question is: did *Geraldine* know that it was fake when she offered it to us? Because if she did, I'm going to have some very choice words to say to her."

"That's an excellent question," I said, "but I don't think we're going to get any answers until morning."

A loud knocking on the front door startled us. Well, it startled me. Curtis looked like he might be biting back some choice words of his own.

"That'll be the patrol car. Could have used them earlier." He stomped out of the garage in the direction of the front door.

"More visitors." Aunt Evie smoothed a hand over her hair. "I haven't seen this much action after midnight since Andy died."

Jack laughed and I shook my head. I did *not* want to imagine what kind of late-night action my aunt and uncle had gotten up to.

"Let's get back to that cup of tea," I said firmly.

Curtis led two police officers into the kitchen a

moment later. One of them had been at the ball. Aunt Evie's tiny kitchen was getting very crowded with seven of us in it. Aunt Evie and I sat across from the two officers, Priya and Jack leaned against the wall, and Curtis paced back and forth in the confined space like a caged lion dreaming of the savannah.

Fortunately, it didn't take them long to get Aunt Evie's statement, since she hadn't actually seen the intruder. Curtis had already established that the man had got in by forcing open the back door and the more senior officer suggested that Aunt Evie replace it with something more secure.

"These sliding doors are surprisingly easy to get open if you know what you're doing," he said. "Most of them just lift right off their tracks."

He gave her the name of a local company that made security doors and promised to send a technician around in the morning to dust for fingerprints, though he wasn't very hopeful of getting any useable prints, given how many of us had been in and out in the meantime.

"We think the intruder was after the necklace in Aunt Evie's safe," I said. "But only two other people knew it was here."

I explained the situation, but the officer seemed unimpressed, taking Aunt Evie's view that both Greta and Geraldine could have found easier ways to grab the necklace than breaking into Aunt Evie's house in search of it.

"It was probably just a run-of-the-mill break-in," he said. "No reason to think they were after anything in particular."

Then he got a description, such as it was, from Jack and Priya, and the two officers left.

"We should probably think about leaving, too," Priya said. "You should try to get some more sleep."

"I don't think I'll sleep a wink after all this," Aunt Evie said.

"Do you want me to stay?" I asked. "I could sleep in the spare room."

She'd done the same for me when I'd had my accident.

"No, of course not. I'll be fine." She flapped her hands at us in a shooing motion, as if we were a flock of chickens. "You young people are having a nice night together. Go back to your party."

"I think I'm all partied out," Jack said. His tall frame drooped against the wall and I felt a twinge of guilt for keeping him out so late. Shift work really messed with his sleep schedule. He shot me a grin. "Our Monday night pizza nights aren't usually this dramatic."

Priya smothered a yawn. "And I've got to get up in—" She checked her watch. "Six hours for work. Come on, people, the party's over."

"Are you sure you don't want me to stay?" I asked.

"*I'll* stay," Curtis said. "If that guy comes back, neither of *you* will be able to stop him."

"Oh, but you don't need to—" Aunt Evie began.

"Your back door wouldn't keep out a stiff breeze," Curtis said firmly. "Tomorrow you can get a new one, but I'm staying tonight." He fished his car keys out of his pocket and held them out to me. "Take my car and drive the others back. You haven't drunk much."

They were warm from his body heat. I eyed him doubtfully. It seemed like an imposition, but I couldn't deny it made me feel better to know my aunt would have someone on hand who could handle any more intruders.

"Are you sure?" I asked.

"About letting you drive my car?" He pretended to misunderstand me. "It could be a disastrous mistake. I may never speak to you again if you crash it."

I rolled my eyes. "About staying. Aunt Evie's spare bed is more lump than mattress."

He shrugged. "I've slept on worse."

In the flurry of goodbyes, Aunt Evie whispered in my ear, "This one's a keeper."

I only smiled, but in my heart, I had a feeling that she was right.

CHAPTER 24

I WAS BACK AGAIN NEXT MORNING, BRIGHT AND EARLY. I PARKED Curtis's car in the driveway and let myself in with my key. As I strode down the hallway to the kitchen, Curtis came out of the bathroom with a towel wrapped around his waist.

"Oh, wow." I hardly knew where to look. I mean, I knew where I *wanted* to look. That muscled chest was a vision of perfection. I could see men wearing far less on the beach any day of the week, but somehow this was different. This was *Curtis*.

"*Wow*?" He grinned at me and I felt heat sweep up my face in a rush.

"I said that out loud, didn't I? For goodness' sake, put some clothes on. You're too distracting."

Smiling like a cat that had got the cream, he whisked himself into the spare bedroom and shut the door.

"Charlie?" Aunt Evie called from the kitchen. "Is that you?"

I went in and gave her a hug. "Good morning. How did you sleep?"

"Like a log. Having that hunky policeman of yours sleeping in the next room made me feel very safe. What kind of muesli do you think he'd like for breakfast? Or should I make him an omelette? I have tomatoes and I think some herbs in the fridge."

I put the kettle on while she fussed around checking her vegetable drawers.

"I have no idea what he eats for breakfast."

She straightened and shot me a mischievous look. "You should do something about that."

I fully intended to, but adult "sleepovers" might still be a little way down the road. We hadn't even managed a proper kiss yet. Too many of our dates seemed to end in disaster.

I got three mugs out of the cupboard and added tea leaves to the teapot while the water boiled. Aunt Evie started chopping tomatoes and a peaceful early-morning calm descended on the little kitchen.

"What are you going to say to Geraldine?" I asked, breaking the silence. "And Stellan, for that matter."

It hadn't occurred to me last night in all the excitement, but this was a serious blow for the fundraising efforts of the Yule Ball. There was no question now of Stellan paying the amount he'd bid. He'd been bidding on an intact and valuable piece of jewellery, not a cheap, broken replica. If Geraldine had known the necklace was a fake, trying to pass it off as genuine was a despicable act, even if the money raised was meant to be helping the hospital.

"I'm going to give Geraldine a piece of my mind." Her eyes glinted with determination.

"She may not have known the necklace was a fake."

She stopped cutting to give me a disbelieving look. "You think that rich second husband of hers would have given her a cheap glass necklace and told her it was real?" She resumed chopping, shaking her head. "If I recall correctly, that man was loaded. Why would he do that?"

"Maybe he didn't like her that much. They did get divorced," I reminded her.

"Well, whatever. I can't believe Geraldine didn't know."

"She's always supported the auction in the past, hasn't she? Why would she pull a stunt like this now?"

Aunt Evie pointed the knife at me. "Who knows? Maybe she's done it before. No one actually checked the things she gave us were the genuine article. It didn't seem necessary, when they all came with the valuation certificate."

"We at least owe her the benefit of the doubt. Innocent until proven guilty and all that."

"That's my kind of talk," Curtis said, coming into the kitchen and wrapping his arms around me from behind. "We'll make a police officer of you yet."

I swivelled in his arms and stretched up on tiptoe to plant a kiss on his lips. He smelled of Aunt Evie's soap instead of his usual delicious aftershave but I wasn't complaining.

"I thought you didn't want me to play detective?"

"Who's playing detective now? You already found the necklace." He reached over and stole a piece of capsicum from Aunt Evie's chopping board.

"Aunt Evie and I are going to see Geraldine this morning, to try to get to the bottom of this."

"You don't have to come," Aunt Evie said, head buried in the fridge again as she got out the eggs.

"Oh, yes, I do. *Someone* has to make sure you behave."

"I wish I could come, too," Curtis said. "But I have to pick Maisie up by nine. And given that she's probably had way too much sugar and not enough sleep at the party, she won't be fit for human company today. We're just going to have a quiet day together at home."

"That's okay. It won't take both of us to restrain Aunt Evie." I grinned at her. "Probably."

She cracked an egg into her bowl with a haughty sniff. "You do talk a lot of rot, darling."

CHAPTER 25

A LITTLE AFTER TEN I WAS BACK AT AUNT EVIE'S TO PICK HER UP. She had arranged a meeting with Geraldine, telling her only that we needed her to confirm that the necklace I'd found was truly hers before we spoke to Stellan. My aunt could be cunning like that.

When she answered the door she looked preoccupied.

"What's wrong?" I asked. "Having second thoughts?"

"About accosting Geraldine? Certainly not." She gathered up her handbag and the jewellery box she'd been storing the necklace in. "Let's go."

"You look a bit down," I said as I unlocked my car.

"Just thinking. I had a call from Jim Van Doolen just now."

"Do I know him?"

Aunt Evie had lived in Sunrise Bay for over forty years, and seemed to know just about everyone in the town. I couldn't always keep up with the ever-changing roster of people whose business she liked to fill me in on.

"I don't think so, dear. He's a lovely man. Remember I told you he always dresses up as Santa for the sick kids in the hospital at Christmas and gives out presents?"

"Oh, this is the guy that helps you present the big fake cheque from the Yule Ball at the same time?"

"Yes, that's him. Apparently he's pulled some ligament or other—I didn't quite follow the details—but it means he can't walk. He's on crutches for the next two weeks."

"Oh." I digested this. "So I guess he can't do the Santa thing for the hospital."

"That's right." She frowned out the windscreen, lost in thought. "Who else am I going to get to do it at such short notice?"

I started the car and backed out of her driveway. "You live in a retirement village, Aunt Evie. There must be a dozen jolly old gentlemen here who could take his place."

"But he's so tall! I'm sure Neil would do it, for one, but Neil's tiny in comparison. He'd look like a little kid playing dress-ups in his father's clothing."

"I'm sure you'll find someone." How hard could it be? "You could always pin up the sleeves and the trouser legs if you had to."

She sighed. "I suppose so. Although they do have fur around the bottoms of them."

Poor Aunt Evie. This Yule Ball had caused her even more stress than it usually did, and the stresses weren't over yet. Not that she was one to shy from a confrontation, but I could see how the whole thing with the fake necklace put her in an awkward position. Apart from the hit to this year's money raised, if she put Geraldine into a snit the woman might refuse to donate in future, and Geraldine had been one of the most reliable donors for the Yule Ball since its inception.

Geraldine's house, with its imposing front stairs and its gorgeous vista across the bay, wasn't far from Aunt Evie's. I was soon parking outside.

"Ready?" I asked as I switched off the engine.

Aunt Evie nodded. "Let's do this."

She marched up the massive staircase and rapped sharply on the oversized double doors, a determined set to her shoulders. A kid of about sixteen answered it, all long legs and bony angles.

"Hello?"

"You're one of the grandsons, aren't you?" A little of the wind had been taken out of Aunt Evie's sails as she recalibrated *attack mode* into *exchanging pleasantries with awkward teens mode* on the fly.

"Um, yes?"

I hid a smile. I remembered those teenage years, when talking to strange adults felt like the worst punishment in the world.

"Ryan, isn't it? May we come in? Your grandmother is expecting us."

My ears pricked up. This was Phil's son, Ryan? Greta had been right. He was a beanpole—not the same body type at all as last night's intruder.

"You were a waiter at the Yule Ball, weren't you?" I asked, as we followed him into the air-conditioned cool of a marble foyer with a ceiling two storeys high. I glanced up as we passed under a chandelier that looked like it weighed as much as my car. I hoped it was well secured up there.

He nodded without turning to look at me.

"Do you like working at the Metropole?"

He shrugged. "It's okay."

"Did you see anything odd that night? When the necklace was stolen, I mean?" *Flick any circuit breakers, perhaps?* If he *had* been the one to turn off the lights, who had he been working with?

"Nah," he said to his feet. "I'll get Grandma."

"Not very talkative, is he?" I said to Aunt Evie once he'd left the room.

"Teenage boys rarely are."

Was that all it was? He'd basically fled as soon as I mentioned the necklace. Interesting.

We hovered awkwardly in the foyer until Geraldine appeared. She was wearing a smart suit and a pearl necklace, which seemed overkill for a meeting such as this, but perhaps she had a lunch date. With royalty.

"Come in, come in," she said, kissing the air by Aunt Evie's cheek. "That silly boy should have offered you a seat. But you know boys. So nice to see you, Evelyn. And you, too, Marley."

"It's Charlie," I said. "Does Ryan live with you?"

"He's just come over to fix my computer. He's not just an athlete—he's got plenty of brains, too."

Ah, yes, the track star. So he was fast on his feet. Fast enough to duck down to the fuse box from the ballroom without being missed? Quite possibly. And also, perhaps, a kid in need of some extra cash for drugs. Someone might have paid him to kill the lights—but who was that someone?

Geraldine led us into a room with enormous cathedral ceilings and a sunken lounge. A sweet scent, vaguely familiar, hung on the air. I was so busy gawking at the stupendous view of Sunrise Bay that I didn't notice for a moment that Phil and Flick were both settled in the lounge room. Flick was folded elegantly into a deep leather armchair, one long leg tucked underneath her. She was reading a magazine and barely acknowledged our presence.

Phil was equally unwelcoming. He was wearing a business suit, as if he'd just come from work, and was drinking a cup of coffee with a sulky look on his face. He checked his watch impatiently as we came in.

I glanced uncertainly at Geraldine. "I hope we're not interrupting anything?"

"Well, I do have a lunch date, but I don't suppose this will take long," she said. "Oh, you mean the children?" She gave a fake little laugh and I barely managed to conceal a shudder at the middle-aged Phil being called a child. "I told them the good news last night that you'd found the necklace, and when I mentioned that you were bringing it around for identification today, they both wanted to be here. Goodness knows why. It's not as though they haven't seen it before. Do sit down."

Flick uncurled herself from her chair, reminding me of

a sleek black cat in her tailored black pants. "Would either of you like a drink?"

"Not for me, thank you," Aunt Evie said, and I refused, too. This conversation probably wasn't going to go well, and we might soon be beating a hasty retreat. Best not to get too bogged down in the social niceties.

Phil put his coffee cup down on a side table with a clatter. "What's all this about needing Mum to identify the necklace?"

He scowled at Aunt Evie as if the idea was a personal insult. Charming man.

Geraldine smiled rather condescendingly. "Yes, surely you remember what it looks like?"

She laughed that high, tinkling laugh again, which sounded faker than her so-called sapphire. No one else seemed amused, though Phil's lip did curl slightly. Perhaps that passed for amusement with him. Or maybe he was just constipated.

Aunt Evie extracted the red velvet jewellery box from her enormous handbag. "As to that, there's been a bit of a problem with the necklace. I thought it best to be sure we were dealing with the real thing."

Geraldine frowned. "Whatever do you mean?"

Flick sat forward in her chair, apparently eager to see the necklace again. I wondered where Ryan was. Maybe he turned off the lights so *she* could steal it, and I'd just been wrong about Tim's involvement. She still had the best motive. She wanted that necklace.

"Ryan's not joining us?" I asked, trying for a casual air.

"I doubt he has the slightest interest," Geraldine said,

looking surprised that I'd even suggest it. "He's probably in the middle of updating my virus protection. You know what kids are like these days. Mad for computers."

You'd think Geraldine, with all her money, could afford to pay a proper IT person rather than leaning on her grandson for computer support. Still, perhaps that was my dislike of Geraldine talking. For all I knew, she *was* paying Ryan.

She turned back to Aunt Evie, who was still clutching the jewellery box. "You were saying there's a problem?"

For answer, Aunt Evie opened the lid of the box, which was angled so that only Geraldine could see the contents. Geraldine drew in her breath sharply.

"What?" She looked up uncertainly at Aunt Evie, the beginnings of a storm brewing on her face. "I don't understand. You *broke* it? You never mentioned it was broken."

Flick was off the couch and at her mother's side so fast I barely saw her move. "The setting's broken?" And then she saw it. Aunt Evie had packed all the little splinters of blue glass we could find into the jewellery box with the golden chain and the Argyle diamonds surrounding the empty setting.

Flick's face was a picture at seeing dear old dad's gift to her mother basically trashed. But neither of them seemed to understand what it meant.

Phil was on his feet, too, and I could see from his face that he, at least, had an inkling of what was up.

"That was a Ceylon sapphire," Geraldine said, surveying the blue shards with an outraged expression.

"What on earth happened? Did someone back a *truck* over it?"

From the look on her face I guessed she would rather like to back a truck over whoever had done this to her precious necklace.

"Geraldine," Aunt Evie said gently, "I don't think it *was* a Ceylon sapphire."

CHAPTER 26

Flick's brows snapped together in a furious frown. "Are you suggesting that my father tried to dupe my mother with a piece of *glass*?"

"I'm not suggesting anything," Aunt Evie said. "I'm only showing you the proof that it wasn't what you thought it was. I have no idea if the necklace has been a fake since the beginning or not."

"But that's not possible," Geraldine said. "I had the necklace revalued a couple of years ago. You remember, don't you, Phil? Phil offered to take it to a jeweller friend of his. He would certainly have noticed if the sapphire wasn't genuine."

"That's right," Phil said, though he wasn't quite as vehement as the two women.

In fact, Phil wasn't looking as surprised as Geraldine and Flick either.

He noticed me watching him and scowled. "The thief

must have ... must have left this replica behind so that the police would stop looking for the real necklace."

Geraldine nodded. "Yes, that must be what happened."

Really? I exchanged a look with Aunt Evie. What a load of balderdash. Even Geraldine didn't look as though she totally bought that theory, and Flick's expression was downright sceptical.

"I thought you told me that the police weren't even looking for it?" she demanded of her mother.

"Well, I suppose the thief wasn't to know how lax the local police are about their duties," she said, but her voice had lost its certainty.

"How would some random thief be able to make a copy?" Flick was like a dog with a bone. "They couldn't do it before the theft, because they wouldn't know what the necklace looked like. And they certainly couldn't do it afterwards, because any jeweller they took it to would surely get suspicious. The police aren't so lax that they didn't contact all the local jewellers about it."

"Wouldn't have to be a local jeweller," Phil said, a mulish look on his face. "They could have taken it to Sydney—or Melbourne. Anywhere."

She rounded on him, hands on hips. "If they were going to run off with it to Melbourne, why even bother coming back? And risk getting caught sneaking around the hotel trying to hide a fake? It doesn't make any sense."

I was still watching Phil, while a number of interesting points occurred to me. Like how convenient it was that his son the track star worked at the Metropole and had been a waiter at the ball. The ball where he'd been so keen to bid on his own mother's necklace.

"So Phil took the necklace to be valued?" I asked casually. Everything clicked into place, and I realised what the scent in the air was. "When was this?"

Geraldine got a vague look on her face. "Ah ... a couple of years ago. Maybe three. I suppose it will say on the valuation certificate."

"Any reason why Phil organised this and not you?"

"Well, because it was his idea," Geraldine said slowly. "He said it was important to make sure that all the valuations were up to date for insurance purposes. And some of them hadn't been revalued since I got them."

"So he took all your jewellery for valuation at the same time? That must have taken a while. How long were they gone for?"

"What does that matter?" Phil broke in impatiently. "It's got nothing to do with the current situation."

His forehead was shiny with sweat. I watched a bead of it break free from his temple and begin a slow slide down the side of his face. It was a hot day, but it wasn't *that* hot. We were in an air-conditioned room.

A room that smelled of the same aftershave that I'd gotten a whiff of when the thief brushed past me in the dark at the Yule Ball.

I took a deep breath. "So if we were to get a jeweller to look at the rest of Geraldine's jewellery, it would all be the real deal?"

Geraldine was aghast. "What are you suggesting?"

"She's suggesting that Phil's a thief," Flick said, giving

her half-brother a disgusted look. "You took it all to your pet jeweller and got him to replace the stones, didn't you?"

Geraldine's face went white and she sat down abruptly.

"Of course not," Phil blustered. "Trust you to assume the worst of me. I know you've never liked me, but this is too far, even for you."

"Oh, yeah?" She squared up to him, hands on hips. "So if I got Mum's diamond necklace out right now and hit it with a hammer, it wouldn't break? How about we try that and see what happens?"

"Stop being such a drama queen," he said.

Frankly, I was on Team Flick for this one. In fact, I'd offer to get the hammer if it came to that. But a glance at Geraldine told me it wouldn't be necessary.

She stared at her son as if she'd never seen him before, betrayal in her eyes.

"She's right, isn't she? That's why you were so insistent on getting everything revalued. It was nothing to do with the insurance."

"I can't believe you're listening to Flick's nonsense," he said.

"And I can't believe you're lying to my face," she snapped. "You needed money for that business of yours, didn't you? It was right around the time when you were trying to buy out that other fellow, your partner ... what was his name?"

"Franco," Flick said. "I remember that. He even asked Irving for a loan, remember? And Irving said no."

That confused me until I remembered that Irving was

the name of Geraldine's current husband, supposedly the richest of all her matrimonial choices.

"And it was right after that that he started nagging you to get your jewellery revalued," Flick finished triumphantly.

"Are you going to sit there and let her make up these lies about me?" Phil asked his mother. "Not even a word in my defence?"

"Philip," Geraldine said. "The only word you're going to hear from me is *disinherited*, unless you sit down right now and tell me exactly what you did and why."

A struggle went on behind his eyes, but I saw the moment he accepted defeat. He sat back down on the lounge opposite Geraldine, looking more like a naughty schoolboy than a middle-aged man.

"Should we invite Ryan in to tell us his part of the story?" I asked, taking a seat on another lounge with Aunt Evie, who was still holding the jewellery box as if it were a bomb. I took it from her and snapped it closed. She was the only one who jumped at the sound. For the other three in the room, the bomb had already been detonated.

Now it was time to face the fallout.

Phil gave me a resentful look that confirmed my suspicions. "Leave Ryan out of this."

But Geraldine was having none of that.

She raised an imperious eyebrow. "What role does my grandson play in all of this?"

"He helped you at the ball, didn't he?" I asked when Phil continued to sit in silence, staring down at his hands. "He turned off the lights so you could grab the necklace." I snapped my fingers as a memory of Phil on his phone in the dying moments of the auction resurfaced. "You texted him to give him the signal."

"Who is this woman?" he asked of no one in particular. "Why is she even here?"

"Never mind who Charlie is," Geraldine snapped. At least she could remember my name now. I must have made an impression. "Is she *right*?"

He sighed. "Yes. But don't blame Ryan. I told him I'd take back the car if he didn't help me out."

Flick glared at him. "You've turned a child into an accessory to a crime."

"He didn't know that," Phil protested, as if that made it better. I supposed it did, in a way. At least Ryan hadn't intended any harm. The poor kid was probably horrified when he realised what his father had dragged him into. "I said I was planning a surprise."

"What about afterwards?" Flick pressed. "When he knew what you'd done?"

"I told him he'd be in just as much trouble as I was if he told anyone what he'd done, and he'd better keep quiet."

Wow. What sterling parenting. I could tell from the look of revulsion on Aunt Evie's face that she felt the same.

"You disgust me," Flick said.

Phil gave a short bark of laughter. "Like that's news."

Flick turned her rage on her mother. "I can't believe you tried to keep me from knowing Tim, because you thought he was after money. And look what your own flesh and blood did."

Was that really the most helpful thing she could have said, considering that Geraldine was already down? Probably not, but I could understand her being peeved.

"I still haven't *heard* what my own flesh and blood did," Geraldine pointed out in a steely tone. "Start talking, Philip."

Did all mothers do that? That thing where they called you by your full name instead of its abbreviation when they were mad? My own mother had been dead so long that I didn't remember, but Aunt Evie sure trotted out the *Charlotte Rose* when she was annoyed with me. It must be universal.

"It's true," he said, still looking down at his shoes as though meeting his mother's eyes was beyond him at this point. "I needed the money to pay off Franco. He was getting ... agitated about it. Threatening to take me to court. Saying that he'd shut me down and bankrupt me if he didn't get his money."

"And you couldn't simply get a bank loan?"

"I was already mortgaged to the hilt. I couldn't have got another cent out of the bank."

"What about selling that ridiculous sports car of yours?"

I was almost starting to like Geraldine. She was relentless. I could see where Flick got it from.

He shifted uncomfortably. "If I started selling off my assets, the creditors would have noticed and started asking questions. Then I would have had even more people demanding to be paid. Besides, what would I do without a car? Catch the bus?"

He said this with an incredulous laugh, as if catching the bus was absolutely unthinkable, on a par with selling off his own organs to raise money.

"So you decided to steal from your mother instead?"

"It was only meant to be a loan. I took the stones and got Eddie to switch them out with replicas so you wouldn't know. I always meant to replace them with real gems one day. Once the business was back on its feet. I figured you'd never even have to know. It was just like a loan, really."

"Except not," I pointed out, "because with a real loan you actually *ask* the person you're borrowing from."

He shot me another venomous look but didn't reply, though I saw the weight of that truth settle on his mother's shoulders. It must be a tough thing to discover the person you've raised and loved their whole life is not the person you thought they were at all. Sympathy for Geraldine welled up inside me.

"And when were you planning on paying back this *loan*, Philip?" she asked. "You bought a holiday house last year. It didn't occur to you to replace my jewels with that money instead?"

"And what about the hospital?" Aunt Evie burst in. She'd been unusually silent, for her, and now it had simply got too much for her. She was practically quivering with indignation. "You've just robbed them of thirty-two thousand dollars. What are they supposed to do now?"

He threw his hands up, in a sort of *what do you expect me to do?* gesture. "I did my best. I tried to talk Mum out of donating the stupid thing in the first place, but she wouldn't listen. And then I tried to buy it at the auction myself, so no one would ever find out that the stones weren't real. But of course Stellan had to jump in and make a big man of himself by outbidding me."

Hmm. That wasn't quite how I remembered things going down. It had seemed to me that Phil had been baiting Stellan, trying to force the price up. Maybe he'd started with the intention of winning the auction, but once Stellan had emerged as his main competition, he hadn't been able to resist getting in a good dig at his old rival. I bet he'd been filled with a warm glow inside at the thought of Stellan unwittingly paying a fortune for a worthless piece of glass.

At least until the hammer came down and inconvenient reality intruded as he remembered how badly things could go for him if Stellan got his new purchase valued and discovered it was actually a fake. And so *Plan B: Steal the Necklace* was back on.

But I didn't bring any of this up. I figured Geraldine was dealing with enough already.

"Go on," Geraldine said, still with that steel in her voice.

"So I had to fall back on the plan to steal it. I had Ryan primed to turn off the lights, if it came to that. All I had to do was get to the stage in the dark and back to my seat before the lights came back on."

"And you hid the necklace in the vase," I said.

"Yes." He looked quite proud of himself for thinking of it. "I thought the police would probably be searching people as they left. I figured Ryan could retrieve it for me later, but those stupid vases have been locked away ever since, and he hasn't had a chance." He glared at me.

I glared right back. "And the break-in at Aunt Evie's house last night? That was you?"

Geraldine dropped her face into her hands. "Oh, Philip. You idiot."

He glanced at her uncertainly. "Yeah. Mum told us Evie was storing it at her house. I thought it would be better for everyone if it disappeared again."

"Better for *you*, you mean," I said. The hide of the man! "So you broke into her house and terrorised an old lady—"

"I'm not *that* old," Aunt Evie objected.

"And terrorised an old lady," I repeated firmly, "committing more crimes to cover up the earlier ones. Real smart move, there, Phil."

"If you'd minded your own business, none of that would have been necessary," he snapped. "But no, you think you're some kind of super sleuth so you had to start poking around."

Flick laughed. "She kind of *is* a super sleuth, you loser. She sure outsmarted *you*. She worked it out and found the necklace, didn't she?"

"Although I didn't figure out Phil was the thief until we started this very enlightening conversation," I said.

"I'm not a thief," Phil said, clearly revolted at being labelled something so crass. "Mum obviously didn't want the necklace anymore if she was so happy to give it away. Even Stellan can't complain. He's no worse off than he was before. I didn't hurt anyone."

"Yes, you did," Aunt Evie said. "You cheated the hospital out of their money."

"I thought the insurance company would have paid out."

"I'd donated it," Geraldine protested. "It didn't belong to me anymore! I wasn't going to put in a claim for a necklace I didn't own."

"How was I to know you'd be such a stickler for the rules?" he asked sulkily.

Clearly he hadn't inherited any of his mother's respect for rules.

"Just as well they didn't," Flick said, "or you'd be up for insurance fraud on top of everything else."

"On top of *what* else?" He threw his arms up in the air. "What are the police going to charge me with? I took my mother's necklace, and now she has it back."

"She has a broken fake back!" I said. "And anyway, that's not the way it works. Just because people recover their stolen goods, it doesn't mean that the thief gets let off."

"And who's going to charge me? My own mother?"

Geraldine said nothing, which seemed to prove his point.

"Don't forget breaking into Evie's house last night," Flick said.

"You've got no proof that was me."

Her mouth fell open in surprise. "You just told us that it was!"

"Your word against mine." He sneered at Aunt Evie.

"And if she ever wants my mother to donate to her stupid ball again, she won't make a fuss."

"Philip Reginald Gottwig," Geraldine said. Wow, now he was *really* in trouble. "How dare you threaten Evelyn right in front of me in my own house? Have you forgotten that you *stole* all my jewellery? Do you think I'm letting you get away with that?"

For the first time, he looked shaken. "But you're my mother. You wouldn't send me to jail for a little thing like that."

Good heavens, the man had no grasp on reality at all. Stealing who knew how many thousands of dollars' worth of jewellery from his own mother was a "little thing"?

"Maybe not," she said. "But my silence is going to cost you." She glanced at Aunt Evie. "*Our* silence."

"What do you mean?"

"Tomorrow you are going to put that new holiday house on the market, and all the proceeds from the sale will go towards purchasing high quality jewels to replace the ones you stole from me. You will also donate thirty-two thousand dollars immediately to the Yule Ball fundraising effort."

"I don't have that kind of money lying around," he protested.

"You'd better find it, because that's the price of keeping this whole affair to ourselves." She raised an eyebrow at Aunt Evie. "If that's agreeable to you, Evelyn?"

Aunt Evie nodded.

"What about *my* silence?" Flick asked. "What do *I* get for keeping quiet about this?"

Geraldine gave her a wary look. "What do you want?"

"Invite Tim to our family dinner on Christmas Day." She stared her mother down. "And make him feel *welcome*."

Geraldine looked distinctly uncomfortable. "He's not ... our kind of people."

Flick's face darkened and I thought she might blow a gasket. "Oh, you mean he's not the kind of person who would steal from his own mother?"

Geraldine persevered valiantly. "We don't know anything about him."

That did it. Flick threw her arms up in the air and let fly. "That's right, we don't. And whose fault is that? I have *two* half-brothers, Mum, and no one's going to tell me I can't see one of them."

"Darling—"

"Don't *darling* me! Do you have any idea what it was like, to have no one in my family who looked like me? The kids at school used to laugh at me and tell me I was adopted because I didn't look anything like my parents. I knew *nothing* about Chinese culture. Nothing about one whole side of my family. And you cared so little about any of that that you gave away the one necklace my father had given you and never even told me I had a brother."

"I cared that your father couldn't even be bothered to leave you a cent when he died. And that woman wouldn't do anything to make it right. Why would I want to associate with people like that?"

"I couldn't care less that he didn't leave me anything. We're rolling in money already! He left his money to his wife, just like every other married person does. And now that his mother is dead, it's Tim's money, and I *still* don't care. *You're* the one who cared."

"It wasn't right. You were his child, just as much as that boy."

"Yes, but maybe Tim's mother didn't cheat on him like you did."

Geraldine's face drained of colour. Poor Geraldine was *not* having a good morning.

"Tim told me all about it," Flick continued. "How you slept with that taxi driver and how heartbroken Dad was when he found out. So much for *growing apart* and that *amicable split* you always told me about. That's the real reason you tried to keep Tim away, isn't it? You denied me the chance to know my own brother, because you didn't want me to find out what you'd done. Your image was more important to you than *my family*."

"Did Tim mention that his father did the same thing to Eileen?" Geraldine asked, regaining some of her fighting spirit.

"I guess Dad was a fast learner. But none of that matters. What matters is that Tim should be part of this family, just the same as Phil." She cast a hostile look at Phil. "He'll be more of an asset than *this* loser."

Geraldine sighed and seemed to fold in on herself. "Fine. You can invite him."

Christmas dinner was going to be one awkward meal for this family. If I were Tim I'd probably run a mile before accepting that invitation, but Flick looked triumphant. "And you'll make him feel welcome?"

"Yes." Then Geraldine's shoulders straightened and she turned back to her son. "As for you—you will give Evelyn a bank cheque for the full thirty-two thousand by close of business tomorrow, or I will be going to the police about the gems you stole from me. And if you truly can't lay your hands on that much cash in a hurry, I suggest you sell that car of yours. I hear the bus is very comfortable these days."

CHAPTER 27

"You're too tall!" I said. "Bend down so I can stick some bobby pins in to hold that hat in place."

Santa and I were in a small break room at the hospital. He crouched enough that I could reach his head. His hat was too small and in imminent danger of sliding off, taking the fake white locks attached to it with it.

"Do you think the real Santa uses bobby pins?" he asked doubtfully.

I grinned. "The real Santa probably relies on the magic of Christmas to glue his hat in place, but bobby pins will work just as well. No one will be able to see them under all the fake fur."

Aunt Evie squeezed into the room with us after a cursory tap on the door. She clapped her hands with glee on seeing Curtis all decked out in his borrowed suit.

"I knew it would fit him! He's a bit taller than Jim, but not much."

"He's also a bit broader across the shoulders," I said,

assessing Curtis with a critical eye. "I hope he doesn't bust out at the seams."

"Like the Incredible Hulk," Curtis said, smoothing his fake beard down over his chest.

"At least you're not green," I said.

"I think it needs more padding," Aunt Evie said. "Curtis, you haven't got the belly. I'll grab a couple of pillows from the nurses."

She whisked herself out of the room, ignoring Curtis's protests, and reappeared a moment later with two plump white pillows, which she proceeded to stuff down his front and back with ruthless efficiency.

He was really way too buff to be a convincing Santa, but it was surprising what a difference the pillows made. If I were a sick kid in hospital I'd be so thrilled to get a visit from Santa that I wouldn't be checking out his physique too carefully. And after Aunt Evie's ministrations, Santa even had a rosy glow in his cheeks, which I found adorable.

"I'm suffocating," he said, flapping his beard to try and raise a breeze. "Are you sure this place is air-conditioned?"

Perhaps the rosy glow was from the heat rather than any embarrassment at being manhandled by Aunt Evie.

"It's only for a few minutes," Aunt Evie said.

Easy for her to say. She wasn't the one sweltering under layers of velvet and fur. Really, it made no sense for Santa to dress this way in the southern hemisphere. Christmas Day was usually stinking hot and we all ate salads and drank cool drinks and complained to each other about the heat. Santa should be wearing shorts and working on his tan, not be decked out in cold weather gear.

"I don't know how these guys that sit around in shopping centres all day doing Santa photos put up with this," he grumbled.

"It's the magic of Christmas," Aunt Evie said sternly, and he subsided, his moment of rebellion over. He really was so good-natured.

We moved out into the main reception area of the ward. Santa and I both carried a sack full of toys, since they wouldn't all fit in one. Aunt Evie toted the giant fake cheque, ready to hand it over to the hospital director.

Priya and a photographer from the *Sunny Bay Star* were waiting there with a handful of nurses and other bystanders. I looked around for Jack, but he must have been busy.

The director made a short speech of gratitude, Aunt Evie handed over the cheque, and then they both posed for a photo with Santa in between them, beaming at the camera. There was a smattering of polite applause, and then it was time for Santa to make the rounds of the ward.

I trailed along behind, watching as he stopped at each bed to hand over a present and have a little chat. He was a natural with the kids, ho-ho-hoing as if he'd been born to the role, making them giggle with silly jokes and listening to their whispered wishes with great seriousness. Even the little ones, who were overwhelmed at first by his size and the suit and beard, were soon calmed by his easy manner.

"Is she your wife?" one little boy asked.

Curtis laughed and assured the kid that I was far too

young and beautiful to marry an old guy like him, and that I was just "Santa's helper".

Finally, he'd made his way around the whole ward. With one last wave and a cheery *ho ho ho*, Santa said goodbye and we left with the happy farewells of the children ringing in our ears. Operation Christmas Cheer was a success.

Aunt Evie and Priya were waiting for us. Curtis wrenched off the hat and its attached snow-white locks as soon as the doors swung shut behind us. His dark hair lay flat against his head with sweat.

"You look like you could do with a Christmas beer after that," I said.

"I like the way you think," he said. "Although the true Christmas miracle will be getting out of this suit."

"How did it go?" Aunt Evie asked.

"Great," I said. "The kids loved him."

"I think they were more interested in the presents than me," Curtis said.

Jack hurried in, dressed in his blue scrubs. His usual cheerful smile was missing as he went straight to Priya.

"What's wrong?" she asked as soon as she saw the look on his face.

"Rose just came on-shift, and she told me she went to the doctor this morning."

I remembered Jack's friend Rose from our joint housewarming party. She was a friendly, motherly woman.

"Is she okay?" Priya asked.

"She was just getting a new prescription," Jack said.

"The thing is—your mum is her doctor and they got chatting."

Oh, no. I could see where this was going. Priya could, too, judging by the look on her face.

"Rose was very surprised when your mum mentioned that we were going out, because I hadn't said anything. And then the subject of how we met came up, and Rose told her that I only started working here three weeks ago, so I couldn't possibly have been here when Charlie was in hospital in October." He looked miserable. "I'm sorry. We've been sprung."

Priya shrugged, as if she didn't care. I doubted any of us were convinced. "That must be why Mum's been calling me for the last half-hour. Good thing I didn't have time to take her calls. I'll think of something before I call her back."

"If there's anything I can do ..."

She laid a hand on his arm. "Don't worry. It'll be fine."

"You'd better tell her the truth," I said, nobly refraining from saying *I told you so*. I'd been convinced Priya's lies would come back to haunt her, but this wasn't the time for that.

"Yes," Aunt Evie said. "You'll only make it worse if you don't."

Priya drew in a deep breath, then smiled brightly. "Well. That's a problem for later. Hey, Santa. There's some mistletoe over here. Why don't you and Charlie pose for another photo for the paper?"

The mistletoe was tacked up in the middle of a tinsel-draped doorway.

"Good idea," Aunt Evie said, giving Curtis a little push in the right direction. It was like watching a chihuahua trying to herd a Great Dane. She nodded at me. "Go on."

"I'm sure you don't need any more photos." I was fine with Priya distracting herself with work, but I didn't see why mistletoe had to be involved. "And why do I have to be in it?"

"You're Santa's helper," Priya said.

The hospital director, accompanied by Priya's photographer, emerged from the children's ward, looking very pleased. Suddenly everyone's attention was on her and Priya started an impromptu interview.

For the moment, Curtis and I were alone under the mistletoe.

He looked up at it, then back down at me with a mischievous grin on his face. "Seems a shame to waste it."

I laughed. "I don't kiss men with beards."

He pulled it off. "Ah, that feels better." His dimple peeked out. "What's your position on kissing men in red suits?"

I moved closer, resting my hand on his broad chest. "I'm not sure I have a position on that. Can I get back to you?"

His smile broadened. "I suppose your people could get in touch with my people. Or ..."

My heart beat kicked up a notch. His lips were very close. "Or?"

"Or we could give it a whirl and see what we think." He bent closer, his breath mingling with mine. "I've been dying to kiss you properly for so long."

"Mmmm." I'd meant to say, *Me too*, but suddenly I was in the middle of the best kiss of my life, and I couldn't quite remember how words worked. So much for waiting for the perfect time for our first real kiss. It turned out that the perfect time was *now*.

I heard the click of a camera shutter and saw a flash through my closed eyelids. My eyes flew open to find the photographer beaming at us.

"Can we try that again, *with* the beard and the hat this time?" he asked. "That would make a great shot for the front page of the Christmas edition."

My mouth fell open in horror, but Curtis only laughed. "Sorry, mate. No photos. Mrs Claus wouldn't approve." Then he leaned closer and whispered, "Besides, we need more practice. We probably should try that again a few hundred times."

I smiled. "We might need to devote weeks to perfecting our technique."

"I'm game if you are."

I sighed with pure happiness as his lips found mine again.

In the background, I heard Aunt Evie say in a tone of great contentment, "Finally! That's the *real* Christmas miracle."

IF YOU WOULD LIKE to read an exclusive free story about Charlie and the gang and the Great Pavlova Debacle, plus hear about new releases, special deals and other book

news, sign up for my newsletter at www.
emeraldfinn.com.

Reviews and word of mouth are vital for any author's success. If you enjoyed *Santa, Surf and Sapphires*, please take a moment to leave a short review at Amazon.com. Just a few words sharing your thoughts on the book would be extremely helpful in spreading the word to other readers (and this author would be immensely grateful!).

Come and chat with me and other cozy mystery lovers in the friendly Facebook group A Pocketful of Cozies. We'd love to have you!

THE LIFE'S A BEACH SERIES

   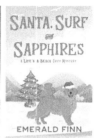

Welcome to beautiful Sunrise Bay, where the beach is hot and the corpses are cold.

When Charlie Carter catches her fiancé cheating with her best friend, she swaps power suits for swimsuits and moves to the idyllic seaside town of Sunrise Bay, home of her feisty retired aunt. Maybe a dose of vitamin sea can cure her broken heart.

Everything is going swimmingly until Aunt Evie's book club pal Peggy turns up deader than Charlie's engagement. Aunt Evie is convinced it was murder. Charlie's not convinced, but the more she discovers, the more she suspects that Aunt Evie is right, as usual. Now Charlie, with the help of one inquisitive four-legged neighbour, must use her keen photographer's eye to spot the killer ... before they take her out of the picture.

See the Life's a Beach series on Amazon

Acknowledgements

Thanks, as always, to my husband Mal for his beta reading and unfailing support of my writing.

Once again, my dear friend Jen Rasmussen has saved me from making an idiot of myself with her excellent editing and smart story suggestions, and I am truly grateful.

About the Author

Emerald Finn loves books, tea, and chocolate, not necessarily in that order. Oh, and dogs. And solving mysteries with the aid of her trusty golden retriever. No, wait. That last bit might be made up.

In fact, Emerald herself is made up, though it's absolutely true that she loves books, tea, chocolate, and dogs. Emerald Finn is the pen name of Marina Finlayson, who writes books full of magic and adventure under her real name. She shares her Sydney home with three kids, a large collection of dragon statues, and the world's most understanding husband.

Made in United States
Orlando, FL
03 January 2023

28143452R00157